W9-AVY-782

"If you see anything unusual, call the police first and me second."

"I'll be fine," Darcie said. "Thanks again."

She was aware that Caleb stood watching her head for her car for a moment before turning toward his own vehicle.

What a complex man he was—so much more considerate and caring than she'd have expected at first glance.

As she crossed the lot, she balanced the leftovers on one hand while rooting in her purse for her keys with the other. She lifted her hand for a final wave, which Caleb returned as he slid into the cab. She stepped into the shadows and reached for the door handle.

A hand from behind clamped over her mouth. At the same moment, a strong arm wrapped around her, pinning her arms to her body. The salad dropped to the asphalt, and she was jerked roughly backward, deeper into the darkness of the van's shadow.

Books by Virginia Smith

Love Inspired Suspense

Murder by Mushroom
Bluegrass Peril
A Taste of Murder
Murder at Eagle Summit
Scent of Murder
Into the Deep
A Deadly Game
*Dangerous Impostor
*Bullseye
*Prime Suspect

Love Inspired

A Daughter's Legacy

*Falsely Accused

VIRGINIA SMITH

A lifelong lover of books, Virginia Smith has always enjoyed immersing herself in fiction. In her mid-twenties she wrote her first story and discovered that writing well is harder than it looks; it took many years to produce a book worthy of publication. During the daylight hours, she steadily climbed the corporate ladder and stole time to write late at night after the kids were in bed. With the publication of her first novel, she left her twenty-year corporate profession to devote her energy to her passion—writing stories that honor God and bring a smile to the faces of her readers. When she isn't writing, Ginny and her husband, Ted, enjoy exploring the extremes of nature—skiing in the mountains of Utah, motorcycle riding on the curvy roads of central Kentucky and scuba diving in the warm waters of the Caribbean. Visit her online at www.virginiasmith.org.

PRIME SUSPECT

VIRGINIA SMITH

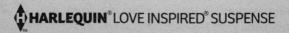
HARLEQUIN® LOVE INSPIRED® SUSPENSE

If you purchased this book without a cover you should be aware
that this book is stolen property. It was reported as "unsold and
destroyed" to the publisher, and neither the author nor the
publisher has received any payment for this "stripped book."

Recycling programs
for this product may
not exist in your area.

™ LOVE INSPIRED BOOKS

ISBN-13: 978-0-373-67554-8

PRIME SUSPECT

Copyright © 2013 by Virginia Smith

All rights reserved. Except for use in any review, the reproduction
or utilization of this work in whole or in part in any form by any
electronic, mechanical or other means, now known or hereafter
invented, including xerography, photocopying and recording, or in
any information storage or retrieval system, is forbidden without
the written permission of the editorial office, Love Inspired Books,
233 Broadway, New York, NY 10279 U.S.A.

This is a work of fiction. Names, characters, places and incidents are
either the product of the author's imagination or are used fictitiously, and
any resemblance to actual persons, living or dead, business establishments,
events or locales is entirely coincidental.

This edition published by arrangement with Love Inspired Books.

® and TM are trademarks of Love Inspired Books, used under license.
Trademarks indicated with ® are registered in the United States Patent
and Trademark Office, the Canadian Trade Marks Office and in other
countries.

www.LoveInspiredBooks.com

Printed in U.S.A.

There is a time for everything, and a season
for every activity under the heavens.
—*Ecclesiastes* 3:1

This book is dedicated to Sloane Stoklosa.

Thank you for having such a great name,
and letting me use it in a book!

Acknowledgments

This book could not have been written
without the assistance of two very special people.
Anna Zogg, a talented writer and wonderful editor,
helped me when I was stuck and gave me two ideas
that springboarded me into the story. My mom,
Amy Barkman, encouraged me throughout the
writing with her unwavering faith in Caleb's story.
Thank you, thank you! I also appreciate
Mr. Tom Chatham, CEO of Chatham Created Gems,
Inc., for answering my questions and recommending
resources for research. And as always, I am honored
to be able to work with Tina James, who is so
much more than an editor. She is involved from
the beginning of every book all the way to the end,
and her expertise makes the stories better. I'm also
grateful to my awesome agent Wendy Lawton.

ONE

Almost two dozen windows in the rear facade of the sprawling antebellum mansion looked out over the pool deck, any one of them potentially concealing a hidden watcher. Darcie Wiley suppressed a shudder at the idea of a pair of eyes spying on her from behind one of those spotless panes of glass. Mrs. Byler may very well be in one of those rooms, watching. From the moment Darcie had arrived at Fairmont Estate that morning, the housekeeper had made no attempt to mask her dislike of Mr. Fairmont's newest employee.

What do I care? This job is only temporary anyway. As soon as I can find something better, I'll get out of her way.

But beneath the brave mask she kept in place, Darcie did care. Mrs. Byler's dislike rubbed at feelings raw from grief, and more than once today tears had blurred Darcie's vision. Like now.

Blinking furiously, she deposited the kitchen trash bag into the garbage bin and then latched the lid. Between her and the mansion's rear patio lay an elaborately landscaped pool deck, bright June sunlight glittering off the crystal water. Lovely but somehow out of place in the backyard of a pre–Civil War era mansion. Behind her, on the other side of the pool deck, stood a long one-story building. The pool house, at least, matched the setting. Care had been taken with the architecture to ensure that regardless of its modern purpose, the building looked like part of the original estate.

A familiar noise sounded in the distance. The high-pitched yap of a dog. Darcie's ears pricked to attention. Within seconds, dozens of other canine voices joined the first. A smile stole across her lips. They sounded exactly like her darling Percy. The famous Fairmont Kennel must be somewhere nearby. Judging by the direction of the barking, perhaps even just behind the pool house.

She glanced at the mansion's windows. Mrs. Byler would accuse her of shirking her duties if she didn't return to the kitchen immediately and put away the silver she'd spent hours polishing that morning. But surely she deserved a short break. And suddenly she really wanted to see the birthplace of the animal that had given Mama so much joy in the last torturous months of her life.

With another glance toward the windows, she headed around the side of the pool house with a quick step. When she rounded the corner, she stopped in surprise. A man was stooped on the ground, his broad back turned her way. She must have made a sound, for he turned. When he caught sight of her, he rose to his feet. For an instant Darcie fought an instinct to run. His muscular build, massive shoulders and intimidating height would give anyone pause, even without the colorful array of tattoos decorating his forearms. But the friendly smile that lit his face halted her.

He spoke in a pleasant baritone as warm as his smile. "Hello."

"Uh, hi." She gave a nervous laugh. "You startled me. I wasn't expecting to find anyone here."

"Another minute and you wouldn't have. I just finished cleaning up." He held up a paintbrush, and she saw that he had been kneeling by a faucet. The grass beneath the spigot was wet and whitewashed, and a paint tray lay upside down within arm's reach. The dogs began barking again, much closer this time. The man cocked his head in that direction. "I've been hearing those yappers all day. Sure sounds like a bunch of 'em."

"I thought so, too," Darcie said. "I was on my way to see them."

She headed toward the corner, making an arc around him. When she drew even with him, he tossed the paintbrush on the pan and fell in beside her.

"Might as well take a look, too. My name's Caleb, by the way."

Suddenly uncomfortable, she avoided his friendly gaze by looking straight ahead. She'd never been entirely comfortable around unknown men. Or ones she knew, either, for that matter. But she couldn't be rude, could she? "I'm Darcie."

When they rounded the corner, she saw immediately why the barking sounded so loud. The kennel, a long single-story building, ran perpendicular to the pool house. On the far side stood a barn-shaped building with garage doors. In a fenced area that ran the length of the kennel, at least a dozen balls of white, fluffy fur frolicked in the grass. A pair of larger dogs dozed in the shade nearby.

Darcie's heart melted at the sight of the puppies that looked so much like her own Percy. "Oh, look at them! How adorable." She hurried over to the fence, delighted when the puppies ran and tumbled toward her. She stuck her fingers through the chain links and was rewarded by a dozen wet tongues vying to greet her with doggy kisses.

"They look like overgrown, furry rats with no tails."

She glanced up to find Caleb staring down at the darlings with something that resembled a perplexed scowl.

"Trust me," she told him, "they're not rats. They're very expensive dogs."

"Hmm." He didn't sound convinced. "Well, at least they're not like that one."

She looked where he pointed. In the fenced yard at the far end of the kennel stood a much larger animal, its eyes fixed on them. A rottweiler.

"This morning Mrs. Byler mentioned something about a guard dog who roamed the estate grounds at night. That must be him." She laughed. "These little babies wouldn't be much use as protection."

With a final caress of soft puppy fur, she rose and looked toward the narrow breezeway that connected the kennel to the pool house, where a door stood cracked open. Maybe an office of some sort? "I wonder if we'd be allowed to hold one." She headed toward the door.

Caleb shook his head as he walked beside her. "You mean people actually pay money to buy a dog the size of a guinea pig?"

Darcie couldn't hold back a chuckle. "They do grow bigger than that."

Once at the door, she knocked softly. Complete silence emanated from inside. No one there. Disappointed, she knocked again, this time a bit harder. Maybe someone deeper inside the pool house would hear her and answer. When her knuckles struck the wood, the door creaked open wider, giving her a glimpse of one corner of the office inside. A pair of shoes and a pile of clothes had been tossed haphazardy on the floor just inside the door. Certainly unlike the tidy interior of the mansion.

And then she noticed that the shoes weren't empty. A man's ankles showed between them and the tan cuffs of a pair of pants. That was a person on the floor inside. Was he hurt?

Breath caught in her chest, Darcie grabbed the

door handle and pushed it open farther. The sight that greeted her drove the air from her lungs. A man lay on the floor inside, his neck twisted at an unnatural angle. Unseeing eyes stared toward the ceiling. She knew without checking that he was dead.

"What is it?" Caleb asked from behind her. "Is something wrong?"

She turned to fix a horrified gaze on him. *Call an ambulance. Call the police!* That's what she wanted to say. Instead, the only sound she could force from a throat as dry as the Sahara was a scream.

In Caleb's opinion, Detective Samuels looked far too young to hold a position of such authority with the Georgia State Police. Most of the investigating officers combing the area around the pool house were at least ten years his senior, maybe twenty. But they all treated the young man with obvious respect as they approached the poolside patio table to report various findings. Samuels acknowledged each report with a nod but never took his eyes from the object of his questioning.

Not that Caleb blamed him. Darcie was an attractive woman, petite, with short, silky dark hair and round eyes that appeared larger than usual in her pixie face. And no wonder, after the shock she'd had.

"I moved to Atlanta on May twenty-second," she told the detective. She sat rigid in her chair and stared across the round patio table at Samuels. "I haven't been able to find work, so Mr. Fairmont was kind enough to offer me a temporary job helping Mrs. Byler get the house ready for an important social event next month. Today was my first day."

During Caleb's questioning, he had explained to the detective that he, too, was a temporary employee, hired to do minor repairs and paint the various outbuildings on the estate before the swanky fundraising dinner Fairmont was hosting for an influential presidential hopeful. His pay from this temporary handyman job would cover his rent this month. The Falsely Accused Support Team, his regular job, hadn't received a new client in a couple of months. The work he and his F.A.S.T. buddies did in helping to clear those falsely accused of a crime was important but not very regular.

"Humph." Mrs. Byler, the fourth person seated at the table with Darcie, Caleb and the detective, drew herself up, deep suspicion etched into her features.

Samuels turned his attention on her. "Do you disagree with Ms. Wiley's statement?"

Mrs. Byler's not inconsiderable girth more than filled the patio chair. "All I know is Mr. Fairmont informed me on Friday that there'd be a new girl starting today to help me get the house ready for the dinner. I never had a say in the matter, even though I've managed this house for nearly fifteen years." She cast a tight-lipped glance toward Darcie. "You'd think I'd be given the opportunity to interview applicants."

Samuels turned back to Darcie. "Odd that he

would hire a temporary maid without getting input from the permanent housekeeper. Did you know Richard Fairmont before you applied for this job?"

A deep flush colored Darcie's face. *Interesting.* Caleb saw the detective's eyes narrow as he made note of the girl's discomfort.

"I, uh…" She cleared her throat and stared at the table in front of her. "I've never met him in person, but he is a family friend. He knew my…" Her throat moved as she swallowed. "My mother. She passed away four months ago."

Sympathy washed over Caleb. That explained the deep sorrow he had sensed hovering behind the smile. *Lord, comfort her. She needs Your touch.*

"My condolences." Samuels's smile was plastic and not at all sympathetic.

Mrs. Byler looked ready to burst. She drew herself upright, her full lips pressed into near nonexistence. "And what were you doing at the kennel, I ask you?" She leveled an accusing glance on Darcie. "You had no business there."

"I was—" Darcie's throat moved as she swallowed "—taking out the trash, and I heard the dogs barking. I wanted to see the puppies."

Mrs. Byler issued another *humph.* "While you should have been working."

For some reason he didn't take the time to explore, Caleb rose to Darcie's defense. "We weren't there more than a minute or two."

The grateful smile she flashed in his direction sent a wave of warmth through him.

Subdued thuds interrupted the tension around the table, and Caleb turned to see a thin, elegantly dressed woman approach from the vicinity of the main house, a business-suited man at her side. Long legs extended beneath a slender beige skirt and matching jacket. An emerald necklace resting across the woman's collarbone against a blindingly white silk blouse sparkled in the afternoon sunlight, and green rays glinted off the deep green studs in her earlobes. When she extended a hand toward the detective, Caleb noticed a matching emerald ring. Whoever this lady was, she enjoyed showing off her obviously expensive jewelry.

"Olivia Fairmont," she told the detective as she allowed him to shake her hand. "My husband and I live here." An elegant hand swept the air toward the mansion. "And this is my husband's financial manager, Aaron Mitchell."

Samuels rose from his seat to shake their hands. Caleb and the women did likewise. The wife of Richard Fairmont. That explained the jewelry. Mitchell, who appeared to be in his late thirties, looked Caleb directly in the eye as he gripped his hand in a firm handshake.

Samuels took the lead, gesturing toward Caleb and Darcie as he spoke. "I assume you know Mr. Buchanan and Ms. Wiley?"

"I don't believe I've made Mr. Buchanan's acquaintance." The smile Mrs. Fairmont directed toward Caleb was polite, but it became frigid when she turned to Darcie. "Of course I know Ms. Wiley. Or, at least, I know *of* her."

Caleb was stunned at the sudden hostility in the woman's voice. Darcie blanched, her eyes going rounder in her face.

Samuels's sharp gaze didn't fail to notice the nuances of the meeting. His eyebrows rose ever so slightly. "Ms. Wiley just informed me that your husband gave her a temporary job, which she started this morning."

Mrs. Fairmont tore her icy stare away from Darcie and gave a brisk nod. "He informed me of his decision over the weekend, before he left on his business trip."

The detective spoke pleasantly. "Ms. Wiley mentioned that your husband is a family friend."

Disagreement blasted from the elegant lips. "Friend? I wouldn't classify the relationship as friendship. My husband employed her uncle for several years, until the man embezzled several hundred thousand dollars from our personal investments. Why he felt any desire to hire a thief's niece, I can't imagine."

Samuels's eyes widened at the revelation. A short, uncomfortable silence followed, during which Darcie's flush deepened, along with Caleb's desire to defend her. So that was the source of Mrs. Fairmont's dislike. It was nothing to do with Darcie, but with her uncle. Caleb was attuned to the small, still voice that he recognized as being the Lord's. And right now that voice told him Darcie Wiley needed his help. If only he knew how.

Mitchell broke the awkward silence. "Mr. Fairmont is out of town until Friday, but I can verify that he did hire Ms. Wiley last week. He asked me to handle the paperwork. Beyond that…" He shrugged.

Darcie shot the man a quick, grateful smile that disappeared when Samuels addressed her again.

"And how well did you know the victim, Ms. Wiley?"

She shook her head. "Not at all. I don't even know who he is. I've never seen him…before." Her eyes squeezed shut, and Caleb knew she was once again seeing the gruesome sight of the man's body.

"His name is Jason Lewis," Mrs. Fairmont said. "He's my kennel manager."

"Kennel manager?"

"He's managed my breeding business for two years. I breed an exclusive bloodline of designer dogs. Maltipoms."

"I'm sorry." The detective shook his head. "I don't know much about dog breeds. What is a Maltipom?"

"It's not a breed." One slender hand rose to gesture in the air as she spoke. The emerald ring winked in the sunlight. "It's a hybrid of Maltese and Pomeranian."

The names meant nothing to Caleb, but then again, the stuff he knew about dogs could fit on a three-by-five card. The list would start with *I prefer cats.*

"I'm sure I don't know what business anyone would have in Jason's office." Mrs. Fairmont shot an accusing gaze toward Darcie.

"Perhaps a tryst," said Mrs. Byler, who hovered near her employer. She stared through narrowed eyes at Darcie, whose spine stiffened at her words.

Her chin rose. "I only wanted to see the puppies."

"I can verify that," Caleb said, glad to be able to offer a word in her defense. "I was with her. We found the body together."

"Ah." Mrs. Fairmont turned a friendlier gaze toward him. "How upsetting for you. For all of us. Detective, do you have any idea what happened? Was it a break-in, a robbery?" A thought occurred to her, and she inhaled a quick breath. "Are we in danger?"

The detective's answer was not reassuring. "It's too early to say. But I promise we'll get some answers. In the meantime, it might not be a bad idea to take extra precautions. Don't go wandering around the property alone, for instance. And if you notice anything or anyone suspicious, call me immediately." His gaze swept the table and ended on Darcie. "Especially anyone you don't know personally."

The girl kept her eyes averted and seemed to shrink into herself. Caleb fought the urge to put a protective arm around her and give her an encouraging hug. He had no more proof than Samuels, of course, but he knew with a certainty deeper than instinct that she wasn't a killer.

Is that how You want me to help her, Lord? Prove that she is innocent of murder?

After all, that's what he and his buddies on the Falsely Accused Support Team did. Maybe the Lord had just given them their next client.

The afternoon had faded into evening before Caleb and Darcie were finally able to leave Fairmont Estate. They'd repeated their "story," as Samuels called it, over and over until Caleb's patience with the detective was exhausted. Thoroughness was one thing, but the interview had become more like the interrogation of a suspect—namely, Darcie.

When Caleb had gathered his painting tools and hurried toward the front of the house, Darcie was just getting in her car.

"Darcie, hold up a second." He tossed his tools into the bed of his pickup and hurried toward where she stood with her hand on the door handle.

"That was pretty rough, huh?" He jerked his head toward the back lawn.

"Yeah," she agreed weakly. "It was rough." She swallowed and attempted a smile. "Thank you for standing up for me back there."

"No problem. I was praying for the right words. For both of us."

A startled expression crossed her features. "You were?"

"Sure. Hey, listen. I don't know where that detective's investigation is going to take him, but I have a feeling you haven't heard the last from him."

Fear flashed into her eyes, and she nodded.

Caleb reached into his pocket and pulled out a card. "Take this. If you need help, give me a call."

Sudden tears glittered in her eyes. "I—" She swallowed and, face averted, opened the car door. "Thanks. Goodbye, Caleb."

Her farewell had the sound of finality. Confused, Caleb stepped back and watched as she started the engine, reversed to turn the car around and then sped down the long driveway without a backward glance. Discomfort stirred in the pit of his stomach as she disappeared from view.

Lord, what was that about? All I did was offer to help.

He started across the smooth blacktop toward his pickup. Apparently she'd rather run away than accept—

His feet halted as though they'd encountered a patch of glue, memories hammering at his brain. There had been another girl he had tried to help who had run like that. Anita. Only when she left, Anita had stolen something he never managed to recover. Money, yes, to support a drug habit he thought she'd kicked. But, more importantly, she had stolen his heart and left a giant, empty crater in its place.

Seeing Darcie flee down the driveway, away from

him, sent all those emotions he'd thought he'd conquered washing over him like a tidal wave.

I can't do that again. I won't. Don't ask me to, Lord.

The only answer to his prayer was a heavy silence as he got into his truck and left Fairmont Estate.

TWO

As Darcie sped down the winding driveway, she couldn't help glancing in the rearview mirror. Caleb stood staring after her, arms hanging at his sides. A lump gathered in her throat. What was wrong with her? Why couldn't she accept his offer of help without feeling like an ice age had overtaken her insides?

The driveway curved around a stand of majestic trees that were probably as old as the estate grounds. She slowed the car to a stop before turning onto the main street, her hands gripping the steering wheel as if it were a lifesaver in a turbulent ocean. She realized she still clutched the business card and was wrinkling it against the wheel. He'd given her his phone number and told her to call if she needed help.

The card read Falsely Accused Support Team. Help When You Need It—Fast. What was he, some sort of professional knight in shining armor? On the back he had scrawled a second phone number and labeled it, "My cell."

A bitter laugh escaped her lips. In her experience, men did not come to the rescue. The last man she'd turned to for help—the only man, in fact—was Mr. Fairmont, and look where that landed her. Whatever had possessed her to contact the wealthy man anyway?

She took her foot off the brake and pulled onto the street. The answer to that question lay buried in a shoe box in the trunk of her car, the box she'd found tucked in the back of Mama's closet. Judging by Mrs. Fairmont's glares, Darcie was no longer welcome on Fairmont Estate. Now she would never have the opportunity to question Mr. Fairmont about the contents of that box.

With a steely determination she'd perfected over the years since Mama's cancer took control of her life, she pushed thoughts of the Fairmonts, the detective, the body and Caleb from her mind and focused on the road.

By the time she reached her apartment complex, her heart had stopped pounding and her mind felt sufficiently numb to face an evening alone. There was always television to banish the silence. And Percy, Mama's little dog, to bring a smile to her face with his antics.

When she turned into the parking lot, she edged past a dark car waiting to exit. For the span of two seconds their windows were side by side, and then the sedan sped into the street. Tires squealed as it zoomed away.

The roar of blood draining from her face left Darcie's ears ringing, and she slammed her foot on the brake pedal. Her car skidded to a halt. In those brief moments, she had caught a glimpse of the driver.

She'd seen him before.

Several times when Mama was sick, she'd spied a car driving slowly in front of the house and felt the creepy regard of watchful eyes. And once she'd seen a man's face through the windshield. Their eyes had connected in the seconds before he had sped away. At the time she'd chalked her irrational fear up to exhaustion from the relentless duties of caretaking.

Now she wasn't so sure. The man she'd seen then was the same man who just driven by. But that was back home, in Indiana. What was he doing at her apartment complex in Atlanta?

It's my imagination. That couldn't be the same man. I'm spooked, that's all. And who wouldn't be, after the day I've had?

Ignoring the chills that raised the hair along her arms, Darcie drove through the lot to the parking space in front of her door. She turned the key and sat in the silent car, scanning her surroundings. Was anything out of place? Everything looked normal.

She exited the car and headed for her apartment. The eleven-year-old girl next door slumped across the four-foot square block of concrete that served as the front porch. When she caught sight of Darcie, she jumped to her feet and raced down the sidewalk.

"Hi, Miss Wiley."

"Hello, Sloane. How are you?"

The girl shrugged a slender shoulder. "Okay."

"Everything, uh, normal around here today?"

Sloane tilted her head, blond locks waving in the slight breeze. "What do you mean?"

If she asked a specific question, it might influence the child's answer. Surely if Sloane saw strangers lurking about it would strike her as "not normal." She shrugged. "I don't know. Anything unusual happen?"

Blue eyes rolled skyward. "I wish. It's been boring, as usual." Then she bounced up on her toes. "Do you want me to take Percy for a walk?"

As though in response to his name, a dog's high-pitched bark sounded from behind Darcie's front door.

The insistent sound dismissed much of Darcie's discomfort. The memory of a dozen puppies tumbling joyfully in the grass brought a smile to her face. "Sounds to me like he'd enjoy that a lot."

She unlocked the door and, with Sloane on her heels, entered the apartment. From the dog kennel just inside the small living room, an ecstasy of yapping erupted. While Darcie tossed her purse on the square, bland sofa, Sloane unlatched the kennel and snatched up the ball of white fur inside.

"He sure is glad to see us," the child said, giggling when the dog bathed her face with an enthusiastic tongue.

Darcie ran her fingers through fluffy white fur and was rewarded with doggie kisses. Oh, how

Mama used to love for her to lift Percy up to her bed so he could snuggle at her side.

Percy had been Mama's dog, a gift from Mr. Fairmont last year when the news of her cancer reached him. Some of those puppies she'd seen today were probably Percy's brothers and sisters. Darcie had remarked at the time that it was kind of the man who, after all, could have held a grudge against them for Uncle Kenneth's betrayal. Mama had agreed and then changed the subject. Percy's limitless energy and constant antics had brought joy to Mama in the last months of her life, and now they did the same for Darcie.

She picked up the retractable leash from the otherwise empty coffee table and handed it to the girl. "Take him out quickly. Poor little guy has been cooped up all day. This is the longest he's ever had to go without a walk."

Sloane clasped the hook onto Percy's collar and headed toward the open door. In the doorway she turned.

"You know, you ought to unpack sometime. It looks pretty awful in here."

The door slammed shut behind her, leaving Darcie alone in the empty apartment. She glanced around the room. A sofa of nondescript color rested against one wall, a matching chair opposite. In between there was a cheap coffee table with nothing on its surface. A television set, one of the old, heavy ones, rested on an inexpensive stand. All standard-issue for an apartment that had been advertised as furnished. Besides that, she only had her DVD player—sitting atop the TV set but not yet hooked up—and a couple of cardboard boxes that she hadn't unpacked stacked in the corner. Mingled with her things inside were Mama's, and she hadn't been able to make herself unwrap them, to set them in their new home in an alien landscape.

The child was right. It looked awful in here. Awfully sad. Awfully lonely. What she needed was a friend, someone to help her ease into this new life without Mama. Unbidden, Caleb's image rose in her mind, but she pushed it away. No, not a man. Definitely not.

She sank onto a couch cushion, and her head dropped into her hands. The events of the day had stirred up all the emotions she thought she'd conquered in the past few weeks.

It was the body. Again, the sight of the dead man loomed in her mind, and she gave in to an uncontrollable shudder. She'd seen dead people before. Hadn't Mama died in her arms? But today was different. This man had died as a result of violence, and that violence was apparent on his purpled face, in his bulging eyes. Accusing eyes, as though in their dying moment they had fixed on the one who had forever robbed their owner of life and happiness. Not dissimilar, in fact, to the eyes Mrs. Fairmont had turned on her.

And then there were Caleb's eyes.

Darcie shook her head. Why, among all the eyes she'd seen today, were Caleb's eyes the hardest to ignore?

Oh, Lord, I—

The half-formed prayer halted. She'd given up praying months ago. What good did it do to pray to someone who didn't hear and didn't answer?

Something caught her attention. Moving slowly, she rose and skirted the coffee table toward the stack of boxes in the corner. Was she imagining things? Her memory had played tricks on her lately, victim to the numbness that she gathered around her emotions like a shield. But how could she imagine the telltale sign of a piece of fabric hanging loose from one of the boxes that was supposed to still be sealed? The familiar pattern taunted her from across the room. A brightly colored quilt, the same one that had covered Mama's bed last winter as she lay dying. It had been on the bottom of the box, a cushion for the framed pictures and glass bric-a-brac that Mama had kept close in her last days. How, then, could it hang loose from the folds at the top of the box?

A horrible suspicion stole over her. Had that man in the car been inside her apartment? Gone through her things? Or was it, perhaps, someone else? Someone still here?

Heart pounding, she tiptoed forward and, with a quick movement, threw open the closet door. Empty. She looked into the kitchen and then crept down the short hallway. Glanced into the empty bathroom. Inspected the bedroom closet, also empty. Carefully stooped down to look beneath the bed. The linen closet was small enough that no one could hide there, but she checked it anyway.

Only when she had examined every window and ensured that all the locks were engaged and every pane of glass was unbroken did she finally allow herself to draw in an easy breath. Everything was secure. She was safe.

But one thing was sure. That quilt in the box had not moved of its own accord.

Caleb's phone rang as he pulled his burger and fries from the take-out bag. He dove for the kitchen counter and managed to snatch the phone just before voice mail took over.

"Hello?"

At first he thought the caller had hung up. After a pause, an unsteady female voice said, "Caleb, is that you?"

He placed the voice immediately and straightened, the phone to his ear. *Darcie.* And she sounded upset. Surely the detective hadn't filed charges against her already. "What can I do for you, Darcie?"

"I—you said to call if I needed help. I think I do."

A million thoughts battered Caleb's mind. Why had he given her his phone number? If she wanted to hire the Falsely Accused Support Team he should have let her follow normal channels. The contact information printed on the card would have put her in touch with Mason, who screened all prospective clients. The task had fallen on him because, of the three members of F.A.S.T., he was the most intuitive. Mason could spot a fake within minutes, whereas Caleb's heart was the consistency of warm Play-Doh, soft and pliant and completely moldable. Especially when it came to women who needed help.

I should tell her to call Mason. He knows all the right questions to ask.

He found himself saying, "Tell me what's wrong."

"It's probably nothing. I'm probably overreacting." But her voice wavered on the last word.

Something inside Caleb twisted. "What is it?"

"I—I think someone's been in my apartment. And on the way home tonight, I saw someone. A man. He—he looked familiar. I think he followed me here from Indiana."

He lowered himself into a chair at the kitchen table, letting her words sink in. "Did you call the police?"

Her laugh held a note of hysteria. "And say what? That my door and windows were locked, but I'm sure someone moved my quilt? They'll say I'm paranoid after finding...after today."

True. And they may be right. Completely understandable, of course.

He softened his voice. "Are you sure about the quilt, Darcie?"

"I'm sure! Someone was here, in this apartment. I don't know why, but they were. Maybe it has something to do with that man's death." He heard a quiet sob, and then she asked meekly, "Could you come over? Just for a little while. I need some help reasoning a couple of things out."

Absolutely not. The words were on the tip of his tongue. That afternoon when he had watched her drive away, he'd been reminded of how painful getting involved with a woman could be. Undertaking the task to prove their innocence when they were falsely accused was one thing. He had his buddies to help with that. But going to a woman's apartment alone, when she hadn't even been accused of a crime?

And yet, fear rang out unmistakably in her voice. Fear, the great tormenter. It was not God's plan for anyone to be afraid.

With a sigh, Caleb knew he would help her. More than likely the whole thing was nothing more than the stress of the day playing itself out in paranoia. But what if he was wrong?

But I'm keeping this thing on a strictly nonpersonal level, Lord. I'll listen to her, help calm her down. But that's it.

Hanging out at her apartment was too personal, especially if there was no more evidence to see than a moved quilt. All she wanted was an ear, someone to help her talk this out.

Neutral ground, that's what he needed.

"Tell you what. I haven't eaten yet. Can we meet somewhere for dinner?"

Another pause, and then he heard what might have been relief in her answer. "There's a Mexican restaurant called Taco Cabana on Piedmont Avenue. Do you know where that is?"

He did. "Give me twenty minutes."

"Okay. And Caleb? Thank you."

He sat holding the phone for a long moment after she'd disconnected. Something churned in his gut, something uncomfortable.

"I am not going to fall for this girl." The sentence was aimed at the ceiling and beyond. "I'm going to listen to her and calm her down. Nothing else."

In the ensuing silence, which seemed even heavier after the firm tone of his voice, he glanced at his paint-splattered clothing. Taco Cabana wasn't far from his place. If he hurried, he'd have time for a quick shower first. After all, he might only be offering a sympathetic ear, but he didn't have to go sweaty and covered in paint, did he?

He rose from the chair and aimed a final decision heavenward. "And I'm not paying for her dinner, either."

That settled, he hurried toward the bathroom.

THREE

The Taco Cabana was nearly deserted. Of the dozen or so sturdy wooden tables scattered around the restaurant, only two were occupied. Caleb selected a location along the rear wall, far enough away from the others that their conversation would not be overheard. He was dunking his third tortilla chip in the salsa bowl when Darcie arrived. The waiter followed her to the table and took her drink order as she slid into the empty chair across from him.

When she had settled her purse strap on the back of her chair, she finally looked at him long enough to give him a quick but distant smile. "Thank you for coming." Her gaze dropped to the paper place mat in front of her. "After we hung up I almost called you and canceled."

"Really? Why?"

She shrugged one shoulder. "I started feeling a little foolish. I may be jumping at shadows."

Caleb picked up another chip. "If so, it's understandable. You've had a rough day."

A humorless laugh came out on a breath of air. "That's the understatement of the year."

The waiter returned with her tea, and they placed their orders. When he had collected the menus and gone, Caleb clasped his hands and laid them on the table.

"Are you saying you don't think your apartment was searched after all?"

"No." She shook her head. "I really do think it was." Her lips twisted into a sheepish smile. "But I'm starting to wonder if my judgment is impaired." She leaned forward and looked earnestly into his face. "I mean, I can't think of a single reason someone would go through my things."

Looking into her eyes, Caleb saw that she didn't believe that, not really. Fear still lingered in those brown depths.

"Let's assume for a moment that you aren't imagining things. Do you have jewelry? Cash?"

"Nothing like that. I don't own anything of value."

"Maybe it was a random break-in, then. A thief hoping to find something worth stealing to sell for drugs."

"Wouldn't a thief have broken the door to get in, or a window?"

"Do you have a dead bolt?"

She shook her head again. "Just a regular door lock and a chain, which of course I couldn't latch when I left this morning for work."

Caleb shrugged. "It's not hard to pick a lock."

"But they didn't take anything," she pointed out. "Wouldn't they have taken the television set or the DVD player or something?"

He conceded the point with a dip of his head.

"And besides," she continued, "that doesn't explain the man I saw leaving my apartment complex. I'm positive I've seen him before, up in Indiana hanging around outside my mother's house." She shivered. "He gave me the creeps."

It was possible she had imagined the resemblance to a passing stranger in her anxiety after finding a strangled body. Caleb didn't point that out, though. She was already going through enough self-doubt without his contribution.

The waiter arrived and set two steaming platters of food before them. Caleb noticed the cross hanging from a chain around his neck.

"That was quick. Thanks, brother." He glanced at Darcie. "Do you have a prayer in you?"

The look she gave him was guarded. "Pardon me?"

"Never mind. I'll pray."

He bowed his head and, without seeing if she followed suit, asked a quick blessing over their food and their conversation. When he finished, he looked up to find her studying him with a measuring look.

"So," he said, unrolling the napkin from around his utensils, "if this guy did follow you from Indiana and go through your apartment, that means he's looking for something specific. Something you don't know is valuable, maybe."

"The only thing I have is this." She held up her right hand to show him a ring. Yellow gold, with small green stones inset in the band. "But I don't think it's worth much. It was my mother's, and, trust me, she wasn't wealthy."

Her eyes glimmered with unshed tears, which sent a ripple of sympathy through Caleb.

"I'm sorry for your loss." An overused phrase, but surely there were no words that would truly offer comfort at such a devastating death. While she struggled to regain her composure, he gently changed the subject. "Was it her brother who worked for the Fairmonts?"

The tears dried instantly. She picked up her fork and avoided his gaze by toying with her food. "Yes. Uncle Kenneth was Mr. Fairmont's financial manager. I think he must have had the same job as that guy we met today, Aaron Mitchell."

"And did he really steal from the Fairmonts?"

Forehead drawn with misery, she nodded. "The newspapers said it was about three hundred thousand dollars."

Caleb gave a low whistle. "No wonder Mrs. Fairmont is bitter."

"Yeah, I don't blame her for that." The tines of her fork pushed lettuce back and forth on her plate. "But I think there's another reason she dislikes me so much."

"Oh? What's that?"

"I think it might be because of my mother." She glanced up and then focused her attention on spreading the mound of sour cream over her salad. "A year ago, when cancer started really making Mama sick, Mr. Fairmont sent her a gift. Percy. He's one of those little dogs like we saw at the kennel today."

Understanding dawned. "The dogs Mrs. Fairmont breeds."

She nodded. "I assumed at the time that it was a nice gesture from both of them. Magnanimous, even, considering my uncle. But then after Mama passed, I found the letters."

Caleb paused in the act of lifting a forkful of enchilada. "Letters?"

"Not letters, really. More like cryptic notes. They were in a shoe box in the back of Mama's closet along with a few trinkets. None of them had a date, and only one was signed. It said, 'Per our agreement. Richard Fairmont.' The handwriting was the same in all of them."

He leaned against the chair back, his mind busy. "Sounds like a note that would accompany a payment of some kind. And there were several of these notes?"

"Fifteen or sixteen, maybe." She finally gave up the pretense of eating and set the fork down. "Most of them said, 'I trust you are both well,' or something like that."

Caleb crossed his arms over his chest. "So you

think your mother had some sort of relationship with Mr. Fairmont, and Mrs. Fairmont is holding a grudge against you because of it."

"More than that." She looked up then, and her eyes met his. "I think Richard Fairmont might be my father."

Darcie stepped through the restaurant door into the humidity of a warm Atlanta night, the take-away box containing her uneaten dinner in one hand. They'd solved nothing over the last hour, but somehow she felt better. She had not mentioned the notes to anyone in the months since she had found them, and simply telling someone else of her suspicions had eased some of the tension that plagued her.

Caleb followed behind her. "I still think you should confront him."

"To what purpose?" She turned to face him. "If Mr. Fairmont is my father, he apparently didn't want to claim me for the past twenty-two years. If he'd changed his mind, he would have said something when I called him last week to ask for his help in finding a job. Or at least made an arrangement to see me in person, rather than hiring me sight unseen to be his maid."

Calling him had been a mistake. She knew that now. One she would not repeat. What did she need with a father who wanted nothing to do with her? She was already alone. Best to keep it that way rather than risk the humiliation of being the unwanted offspring who resurfaces when she should have remained quietly out of sight.

Caleb shoved his hands in his pockets. "Are you okay to go back to your apartment? Do you want me to come with you?"

Though she appreciated the gesture, Darcie shook her head. She felt silly for her earlier jumpiness. No doubt she'd fabricated the whole stranger thing in her mind, as Caleb clearly thought. She'd made enough of a fool of herself already. "Thanks, though. And thanks for meeting me."

The restaurant's business had picked up after sundown, and now the parking lot held a handful of cars. The single streetlight had burned out, or been knocked out, so the only light came from the glowing neon signs in the restaurant windows.

"I'm parked over there." She pointed toward her car, which was at the far end of the lot on the other side of a van.

"And I'm over here." He jerked a nod in the opposite direction, toward the pickup she'd recognized when she had arrived. But instead of turning that way, he stood looking down at her. "Promise me one thing."

She had to tilt her head to look him in the face. Red neon lit his features and turned his blue eyes light purple.

"What's that?"

"If you see anything unusual, call the police first and me second."

What a complex man he was—so much more considerate and caring than she'd have expected at first glance. He looked like a thug with that hulking, muscular body and ink covering his arms, but he prayed over his meals in restaurants and called the waiter "brother." Throughout dinner he had paid close attention to her fears and suspicions, but she had sensed a reluctance to reveal anything personal about himself, as though he was determined to keep her at arm's length. And yet, here he was, offering to come to her aid if she needed him.

She wouldn't call him again though. He'd loaned a friendly ear tonight, but she couldn't rely on anyone else to solve her problems. Especially not a man she barely knew, no matter how kind he seemed.

"I'll be fine," she said. "Thanks again."

She was aware that he stood watching her head for her car for a moment before turning toward his own vehicle.

As she crossed the lot, she balanced the leftovers on one hand while rooting in her purse for her keys with the other. Her fingers grasped the keyless entry device. The headlights flashed and she heard the audible *click* of the driver's door unlocking as she punched the Unlock button. Before she turned between the van and her car, she glanced across the parking lot to see Caleb watching from beside his truck. She lifted her hand for a final wave, which he returned as he slid into the cab. She stepped into the shadows and reached for the door handle.

A hand from behind clamped down over her mouth. At the same moment, a strong arm wrapped around her, pinning her arms to her body. The salad dropped to the asphalt, and she was jerked roughly backward, deeper into the darkness of the van's shadow.

FOUR

Panic gripped her even more tightly than the arms that held her captive. For a moment, her brain froze as she struggled to breathe with the rough-skinned hand clamped over her mouth and nose. The sound of the van door sliding open jump-started her thoughts. She was being kidnapped. She had to act, and quick.

Her attacker was taller than she was, and far stronger. The pressure of his fingers against her mouth was intense. Her arms were useless, pinned. But her feet were free. And she was wearing sandals with heels. Short ones, but maybe…

As she was dragged backward, she lifted one foot. With as much force as she could manage, she brought it down on her attacker's, hoping against hope that he wasn't wearing boots. At the same moment, she opened her mouth as wide as she could. The force of his grip pushed his fingers between her teeth. She chomped down.

"Ow!"

The deep-toned exclamation was followed by a string of foul words. For one second, the hand slipped away. Not for long, but long enough. Darcie screamed. She didn't have enough breath in her lungs to produce much volume, and the sound wasn't high-pitched and piercing as she'd hoped. More like a yell than a scream.

But it did the trick.

"Darcie?" Caleb's voice came from across the parking lot, immediately followed by the sound of a door slamming and feet pounding on asphalt.

"Hurry!" said a man's voice from inside the van. The engine roared to life.

Her attacker swung her around, intending to throw her inside. *No!* If he got her into the van, she might never get out. Instinct took over. Her legs rose almost of their own accord and slammed into the van's door panel. Pain exploded in her shin, but the gesture stopped her attacker for a second.

That was all it took. A roar filled the night, and she was released. She fell to the pavement with an excruciating thud. It took a second to recover. Then, scrabbling on her hands and knees, she hurried away. Only when she was out of arm's reach did she turn.

Caleb held her attacker in much the same grip that the man had held her a moment before. His powerful arms wrapped around the thug's body, one across his neck and the other threaded around his arms, pulling them backward at a painful angle. Darcie tried to identify the man who'd grabbed her, but all she saw were patches of white skin around shadow-darkened eyes through a black ski mask. The man jerked sideways and thrust backward to head butt Caleb in the face.

Now that she could get her breath, she screamed again, as loudly as she could. A satisfyingly loud screech ripped from deep in her throat to fill the night.

"What's going on?" The question came from the direction of the restaurant.

"Help!" Darcie shouted. "We're being attacked."

An arm stuck through the van's open front passenger window. Darcie barely had time to register the fact that the hand wielded a hammer before it struck.

"Caleb!"

The big man released her attacker and staggered backward. The masked thug dove into the van's open side panel. With a screech of tires, the van roared out of the parking lot. Seconds later, a pair of men rushed toward them from the direction of the restaurant.

"Are you okay?" one of them asked.

Caleb put a hand to the back of his head. When he pulled it away, it was covered with dark, sticky blood.

He stared at his hand. "Did anybody get the license plate of that truck?"

Darcie would have laughed at the lame joke, but in the next moment, he crumpled to the ground.

"If you won't go to the hospital, you'll need to sign here. This says we aren't liable if you've got a concussion." The EMT thrust a clipboard and pen toward Caleb.

He sat on the rear bumper of the ambulance, an ice pack held to the back of his head. Flashing red lights reflected in the windshields of the cars parked nearby, keeping tempo with the throbbing pain in his skull. Other lights flashed in the parking lot as well, blue ones. Darcie stood near a police car, speaking with a pair of officers, her arms wrapped tightly around her middle.

Caleb signed the paper and handed it back to the man. "Thanks, brother."

He slid off the bumper, wavered on his feet until a wave of dizziness passed and then walked over to Darcie.

Concern colored her features at his approach. "Are you going to be okay?"

"Yeah." He gave a weak laugh. "It's a good thing I've got such a thick skull."

She peered closer. "You've got a thick lip as well."

He slid a finger over his swollen lip. That head butt had brought stars to his eyes, stars that exploded a second later when the hammer had hit him. "I guess that thug's head is almost as hard as mine."

One of the police officers held a pen poised over a small notebook. "What can you tell us about the attacker, Mr. Buchanan?"

Caleb had spent the time when the EMTs were examining his wound recalling everything he could. "Caucasian. A couple of inches shorter than me, I'd say around six feet. One-ninety, maybe two hundred, mostly muscle. Guy was strong as an ox." It had taken all his strength to keep a grip on the struggling man, and Caleb was no weakling.

"Any distinguishing features? Scars or—" the officer's gaze slid over Caleb's arms "—tattoos?"

"Sorry." Caleb shrugged. "He was wearing a black long-sleeved jacket and a ski mask."

"Did you get a look at the second man, the one inside the van?"

He let out a laugh. "If I had, I wouldn't have a goose egg on the back of my head."

Darcie winced before she spoke. "The driver was wearing long sleeves and a ski mask, too. But I only saw him for a second, too quick to even guess at height or anything."

"Did the witnesses see anything helpful?" Caleb jerked his head toward the small crowd that had gathered in front of the restaurant. The two men who had come to their aid stood among them.

The second officer shook his head. "They said it was dark inside the van. They couldn't see anything."

"And no license plate," the first added.

Caleb looked at Darcie. "Did you tell them what you told me about your apartment?"

"Yes." She cast a hurt glance toward the officer with the clipboard. "They think I'm paranoid."

The policeman gave her a kind smile. "Entirely understandable, after what you've been through."

Caleb couldn't believe his ears. "But what about the man she saw earlier, the one from Indiana? And her apartment being searched?"

Yes, he'd been doubtful of Darcie's suspicions before, but surely this attack proved something was going on.

"With no sign of entry and nothing missing?" The officer's skeptical expression said it all.

Caleb directed a question to Darcie. "Did you tell them about the murder victim we found this afternoon?"

The officer answered. "Yes, sir, she did. And we will definitely give Detective Samuels a report of tonight's incident. If he thinks there's anything connecting the two, I'm sure he'll contact you."

The second officer spoke, "We were just about to tell Ms. Wiley that we believe tonight's attack was random."

Caleb threw up a hand in the air, flabbergasted. "I don't believe this. She's telling you she thinks someone has been stalking her, and then she's jumped in a dark parking lot. How could this be random?"

He replied in a calmly rational tone, "Maybe you don't watch the news, sir, but there have been several attacks recently that match this M.O. Women alone at night, getting into their cars. A dark van and two men. Most of the victims have been found dead, their bodies violated and then strangled."

Caleb sobered at the words. Had he stopped Darcie from suffering the same horrible fate?

* * *

The officer's words sent a chill straight through Darcie's core. A strangled squeak escaped from between her clenched teeth. She'd seen a news report about that a few days after moving to Atlanta.

She looked at Caleb. "What if you hadn't been here?"

"Don't think about that. I *was* here."

He moved a step closer to her. For a moment she thought he might put an arm around her shoulders. The thought both comforted and frightened her. She had no desire to get close to this man, or to any man. But Caleb had saved her life.

"I think we have everything we need." The police officer closed his notebook. "If we have more questions, we'll be in touch."

With a nod, both men headed for their police cruisers, leaving her alone with Caleb. Darcie found herself suddenly shy.

"Thank you for coming to my rescue." Simple words, but she meant them from the bottom of her heart.

"Thank the Lord I was still here and had the windows down in the truck so I heard you shout. God's fingerprints are all over that."

God's fingerprints? She bit back a bitter laugh. That sounded like something Mama would say. God didn't concern Himself in the life of Darcie Wiley. The multiple disasters of today were proof of that, not to mention the past few years. How Mama continued to believe in a loving God after all the suffering she'd been through, Darcie couldn't imagine.

But Caleb obviously believed, so out of respect for him she changed the subject. "Shouldn't you be going to the hospital?"

"Nah. All I need's a couple of aspirin and a good night's sleep. I'll be fine." He pulled the disposable ice pack away from his head and rewrapped the bloodstained cloth around it. At least the bleeding had stopped.

"A good night's sleep?" Darcie shook her head. "Good luck with that. I doubt if I'll get any sleep tonight. I might as well not even try."

The look he gave her was full of compassion. "Tell you what. Why don't you stay with a friend tonight? Tomorrow I'll install a dead bolt on your door and we'll get some boards or something to secure your windows. That'll make you feel safer."

Would it? She didn't think she would ever feel safe again.

But it was a nice offer. She managed to give him a grateful smile. "I'd appreciate that. I—" She closed her mouth. Those officers thought her paranoid. Earlier Caleb had said much the same thing.

"You what?"

Something in those blue eyes compelled her to speak. She drew a breath and looked away.

"I know it sounds nuts after what those police officers said about other women being attacked, but I can't help it. I think those men in the van are somehow connected to everything else that happened today. The murder at the Fairmonts'. My apartment being searched. That spooky guy from Indiana."

When he did not reply, she risked a glance at his face. His head was back, his gaze focused on the dark sky. As his silence drew on, she found herself growing anxious to hear his thoughts. Maybe he would say something comforting, something to convince her that she was wrong. She *wanted* to be wrong.

He finally said in a soft, low tone, "I think you're right."

Not the response she'd hoped for. "You do?" Fear crackled in her voice.

He released a sigh and nodded. "It's too much of a coincidence for all those things to happen on the same day. In the same week, even. I don't believe in coincidences. They have to be connected."

As his words sank in, a feeling of dread stole over her. She folded her arms tightly and clutched at her sleeves with suddenly moist palms.

"Then that means tonight's attack wasn't random. They were trying to kidnap me. Maybe even—"

Her throat closed on the words as the horror of the unfinished sentence struck her with the force of a tsunami. *Maybe even kill me.* An image of Jason Lewis's dead, unseeing eyes rose in her mind, along with an equally troubling thought. *They're still out there. And they will try again.*

FIVE

"Call a friend," Caleb advised. "You don't need to stay alone in that apartment tonight, and you're too shaken to think clearly."

She looked absolutely terrified, her eyes large and round above cheeks that shadows made hollow. "I don't have anyone to call. I just moved to town last month. I—I'm all alone."

The urge to gather her into a protective embrace was swift and almost overpowering. Caleb rejected it by shoving his free hand in his pocket; the other was still occupied in holding the ice pack to his throbbing head. Maybe it was he who was too shaken to think clearly. For one moment, he'd been on the verge of offering to take her home with him. That thug's hammer must have scrambled his brains after all.

Lord, what's going on here? Besides being inappropriate asking a woman to spend the night alone in my apartment, that's dangerous territory. She needs help—that's obvious. But I'm not the guy to help her. I already told You, I'm not going there again.

"I should get a hotel room somewhere. I don't

have a lot of money, but anything would be better than spending another night in that place." A shudder rippled through her delicate frame.

Relieved, Caleb nodded with vigor. "That's a good idea. I'll follow you there and make sure you're safe."

The moment the words left his mouth, he knew they were wrong. She'd been through a horrific day, one that would send most people to a psychiatric ward, and he wanted to tuck her in a hotel alone? She would no doubt relive that attack over and over through a sleepless night. Nobody should be alone at a time like this.

A solution occurred to him. She might not have friends, but he did. "You know what? Scratch that. Let me make a call. I have a couple of friends who might be willing to help you out for a day or two."

Hope sprang into her eyes, but in the next moment her shoulders slumped. "It's not only me. I have Percy, too. I can't leave him alone in his crate for several days."

He'd forgotten about the dog. One of those pesky little balls of white fuzz Mrs. Fairmont raised. Caleb heaved a sigh. Even though he wasn't much of a dog person, he couldn't condemn one of God's living creatures to days alone in a box.

"Lauren and Brent don't have a dog, so I'm not sure what they'll say. All I can do is ask." He slid his cell phone out of his pocket, but paused before punching in the number. "Don't worry, Darcie. We'll help you. I promise."

* * *

Alone in her car, Darcie kept glancing in the rear-view mirror. As he promised, Caleb's pickup stayed right behind her the entire way. She forced herself to look at him, and at the road—not compulsively search the surrounding cars for signs of creepy men or a dark van.

Her thoughts returned again and again to the attack. With no effort at all she could feel a strong arm grab her from behind, a calloused hand clamp over her mouth. Her heartbeat kicked up a notch, and she punched the radio button to drown out her thoughts. But no matter how loud she cranked the volume, her mind refused to release her from its morbid review of the day.

Maybe she should call Mr. Fairmont and ask him to help her. He was out of town, but surely Aaron Mitchell knew how to get in touch with him. Whatever the nature of his past relationship with Mama, maybe he'd take pity on her and—

She jerked upright in the seat. What was she thinking? This whole nightmare started because she'd called Mr. Fairmont to ask for a job. That call was a mistake, and she would not make matters worse by repeating it.

With Mama gone—she blinked back tears at the sudden grief that washed over her—there was only one person she could depend on. Herself.

A glance in the mirror showed her Caleb's pickup still directly behind her. Streetlights reflected off the windshield, making it impossible to see inside, but he was there. Could she trust him?

In some ways, yes. She could trust him to be honest. To be kind. To help her out of a quick bind. But trusting someone and relying on someone to solve her problems were two very different things. Reliance made a person vulnerable. She'd never been vulnerable to a man in her whole life, and she couldn't afford to start now.

No, the only thing she could do was leave Atlanta. Go someplace no one knew her. Another big city, perhaps, where it was easy to get lost in a crowd. Chicago. Yes, that's what she'd do. She and Percy would quickly and quietly disappear.

When they approached her apartment complex, she signaled her intent to turn, satisfied when Caleb's blinker came on as well. He followed her through the parking lot, around the first row of apartments to her building in the back of the complex. She pulled into her space and was relieved when Caleb parked behind her. He hopped out of the truck and approached her car.

"Is that your place?" He pointed to the door in front of her.

"Yes."

He held out a hand. "Give me your keys, and you stay here. Lock the door. I'll take a look inside. If you see anything suspicious, lay on the horn."

At least he was taking the situation seriously. Unable to muster a smile, she nodded her thanks as she handed over the keys and then closed herself in. The locks engaged with a click that sounded loud in the silent car. She watched as his large, muscular frame lumbered down the short sidewalk and climbed the concrete stairs in front of her apartment. When he pushed the door open, he paused, his head cocked to listen. Muffled through the car's glass, Darcie heard Percy's shrill bark from inside. Then Caleb entered.

What an odd feeling, knowing a strange man was wandering through her house, looking in her bathroom, her bedroom, her closet.

After a few moments that seemed to stretch into hours, he reappeared in the doorframe and waved for her to come in. A breath she didn't realize she'd held whooshed out of her lungs. Thank goodness there were no attackers in her apartment, waiting for her to come home.

As she stepped out of the car, the door to the apartment next door opened. Sloane appeared, the light from inside the apartment reflecting warmly off of her blond hair. She started down the porch stairs but stopped when she caught sight of Caleb.

Darcie hurried up the sidewalk. "Hi, Sloane. Don't be afraid. This is my friend, Mr. Buchanan."

My friend. I didn't know him until a few hours ago, but he's my only friend. How sad is that?

Rather than fear, the girl's face reflected only curiosity. She said in a clear voice, "Hello, Mr. Buchanan." Without waiting for a response, she turned to Darcie. Excitement bubbled in her voice.

"I've been watching for you to come home. Look what I have!"

Darcie realized she held something in her arms, something white and fluffy. At first glance she thought it might be a stuffed animal. But then it moved, and she realized it was a tiny white dog. "Percy?" She shook her head, confused. How could that be her dog, when she could hear Percy barking his head off inside her apartment?

Sloane giggled. "No, but she looks like him, doesn't she?" She stooped and set the little dog on the grass. With a bark that sounded more like a squeak, it pounced on her shoe and began tugging at her laces.

Darcie knelt down beside her and held a hand out toward the puppy, who sniffed and gave an experimental lick. "She looks just like him, only smaller. She must be younger."

"Mom says we're gonna take her to the vet tomorrow and he'll be able to tell us how old she is and if she's healthy, on account of sometimes dogs in the Humane Society are sick." A delighted giggle escaped the girl's lips when the puppy left Darcie and returned to her shoe. "I don't think she's sick, though. I think she's perfect. I knew the minute I saw her that she was mine."

Caleb made a noise in his throat. Darcie looked up at him and he glanced at his watch, a clear sign that they needed to get going. She straightened. "I think you're very lucky to have found her. What's her name?"

Sloane scooped the dog up and buried her face in soft puppy fur. "Purdy. I named her after Percy, sorta. They can be best friends since they live right next door to each other."

"I'm sure Percy will be thrilled to have a best friend."

Except that Percy isn't going to live here anymore.

With a final wave, Sloane scooped up the puppy, skipped up the stairs and disappeared inside her apartment. Darcie went to her own door, and Caleb stepped aside to let her pass.

He jerked a nod toward the cartons piled in the corner. "Those the ones you think were searched?"

"Yes. See the corner of that quilt hanging out? It wasn't like that this morning."

"Hmm. I've got a buddy who used to be a cop. Maybe he can take a look around and see if there are any other signs we could use to convince the police."

Now that she was here, the apartment held an unspoken threat. Darcie scrubbed down the hair on her arms, which stood at attention. The sooner she got away from here, the better.

Percy's barking became frantic. Poor little guy. He wasn't used to being in his crate when she was home. She stooped down and released the latch, then stood back while he celebrated freedom with his customary race around the room. When he finished the third circuit, he ran to her, rose to place a front paw on her shin as if to say, "Hey! Long time no see!" and then immediately tumbled across the room to Caleb. The big man looked down with a bemused expression while Percy inspected his shoes and the cuffs of his pants. The incongruous sight of the towering, muscular man looking down at a dog that barely stood taller than the tops of his boots brought a smile unbidden to Darcie's face.

"Let me grab a few things. It won't take but a minute." She headed down the short hallway to her bedroom, leaving Caleb in Percy's capable hands... er, paws.

For a woman, Darcie sure traveled light. Either that, or she didn't care much about material things, an attitude of which Caleb approved. Still, it seemed odd that all of her personal items for a short stay fit in a smallish duffel bag while the dog traveled with half a pet store.

He secured the dog's stuff—a bag of food, packages of treats, a cushioned bed, a grocery bag full of toys and an electric water bowl that flowed like a fountain—in the back of the pickup. When he started to lift the hard plastic crate and its canine occupant into the truck bed, Darcie stopped him with a look of pure outrage.

"What?" he asked, crate in hand.

"Percy can't ride in the back. He'll catch a cold."

Caleb bit his tongue on a comment about the pleasantly warm Georgia night. Instead, he opened the cab door and set the crate on the middle of the bench seat. At least it was a small dog. Back on the streets of Vegas he'd seen rats bigger than Percy.

"There." He straightened and turned to her. "Is that everything?"

A look of uncertainty crossed her features. She stared at the dark window of her apartment for a long moment. "I think so."

He held the truck's door wide for her, and she moved toward it. Then she stopped. "Wait. There's something else."

Grabbing her purse, she fished around inside and came up with her keys. With the punch of a button on the keyless entry device, the trunk of her car popped open. The interior contained a roadside emergency kit, Caleb noted approvingly, a set of jumper cables and a shoe box.

Darcie lifted the shoe box slowly, almost reverently, and cradled it for a moment in her arms as if it were a baby. What could be inside that box?

Then he remembered their conversation at the restaurant. She'd found a shoe box of her mom's things, including the letters from Mr. Fairmont. Compassion stirred in his chest. How sad for someone to not know her father. Even sadder to know his identity but be ignored by him her whole life. Caleb couldn't imagine a childhood spent without his father, a strong man of God who cherished his wife, loved his sons and considered it his role in this life to demonstrate God's love to everyone he met. What must Darcie's childhood have been like?

He cut off that train of thought. It was one thing to help out a young woman who needed a friend. Another thing altogether to get carried away by feelings. Hadn't his past proven that to him? First came compassion, and the next thing you knew, you were trailing around after a woman with stars in your eyes and a "kick me" sign plastered all over your stupid self. Like an idiot you were trusting her with the keys to your car and access to your apartment where you kept your spare cash. And then she was gone.

I might have been born at night, but it wasn't last *night. No way I'm going to be suckered twice.* His vow was directed generally in the vicinity of the Lord, but he didn't wait for an answer.

"Okay, anything else?" He spoke brusquely without looking at her.

"No, that's it." The trunk slammed shut with a solid *thunk,* and she climbed into the pickup.

He rounded the front bumper, glancing around the parking lot as he went. Pools of light illuminated the darkness in regular intervals, cast from tall safety lights. Cars filled most of the empty slots. Not a soul moved anywhere.

He slid into the cab and started the engine.

"Your friend didn't mind if Percy came, too?" Was that nervousness he heard in her voice?

He shook his head. "Lauren said she loves dogs and can't wait to meet him."

After studying his profile, she nodded and settled against the back of the seat. Between them, the dog shifted around in his plastic box and then became quiet.

"You don't like dogs, do you?" The question didn't sound like an accusation from a canine enthusiast, thank goodness. Instead, genuine curiosity colored her tone.

Caleb guided the truck out of the parking lot and onto the street. "Let's just say I prefer to hang with humans. Their teeth aren't as sharp."

"Ah, you were bitten."

Without taking his eyes from the road, he took his right hand off the steering wheel and held his arm toward her. "Right there on my forearm when I was ten years old. Twelve stitches, and it left a nasty scar."

Creases appeared between her eyes as she examined his arm. "I don't see anything except ink."

"That's right. When I was eighteen I got my first tattoo to cover the scar."

He came to a stop at a busy intersection and glanced in the rearview mirror at the line of traffic behind him. When he looked her way, he saw a smile twitching around her lips.

"Mickey Mouse?" Her brows arched over laughter-filled eyes that roamed over his tattoo.

"Hey, don't knock the Mouse," he said with mock severity. "He's my childhood hero."

Her laughter bubbled forth. "I'm not knocking him. I watched him, too."

The light changed, and he turned left. Most of the cars behind him went straight, but a few followed. A feeling of unease stirred.

"I do really appreciate you for calling your friend." The worry was back in her voice. "I hope I'm not inconveniencing her too much."

Caleb pressed down on the gas pedal, his gaze switching from the road in front of the car and the headlights in the rearview. The car behind him did not change pace and began to drop away. A couple of seconds later, the one behind that pulled into the left lane to pass it.

"You aren't. Lauren loves having people over. Being a hostess is one of her gifts."

He spoke without looking at her, his attention fixed on the traffic behind him. He was probably imagining things. After all, Darcie wasn't the only one who'd gone through some stuff today. Was he as paranoid as she?

Just to test the waters, he switched on his blinker and made a quick right turn at the next intersection.

"Okay, good." Relief sounded in her voice.

The car slowed, but the turn signal didn't flash. Caleb heaved out a breath. Yeah, like he thought. Paranoid.

Then the car turned right, following him onto the street.

Energy surged through suddenly tense muscles. He tightened his grip on the steering wheel. "Uh, Darcie? Can you figure out a way to strap that crate in?"

She stiffened, her eyes flying to his face. "Why?"

His tone sober, Caleb replied, "Because this ride might get a little crazy. It looks like we've picked up a tail."

SIX

Darcie wrapped the middle seat's lap belt around the crate, then gripped her own seat belt's shoulder strap with unfeeling fingers. "Is it the van?"

"No, a car. Dark blue or maybe black. Two people in the front seat."

She took no comfort from his words. Either her two attackers had changed vehicles or these were two different people. The idea that there might be a whole group after her sent her mind places she didn't want to go.

"What are we going to do?" The words squeaked out through a throat tight with fear.

Caleb replied calmly, "We're going to lose them."

The next instant Darcie was pitched sideways as he executed a sharp right turn. From inside the crate came the sound of claws scrabbling against plastic, and Percy yelped in protest.

Heartbeat thudding in her ears, she was afraid to look. "Did they turn, too?"

His mouth clamped in a grim line, he nodded.

She risked a backward glance. The twin spots of

light behind them looked like normal headlights. Why, then, did they seem to wink at her with ominous intent? She slid down in the seat so her head was shielded from view from the rear. Another turn, this one left, and she was tossed against the door like a rag doll. Her head connected with the glass, but she barely noticed. She focused, instead, on Caleb's face. His eyes moved constantly as his gaze volleyed back and forth.

"They know we're onto them."

"Is that bad?" she asked.

"Well, it ain't good."

How could he speak so calmly? Couldn't he feel the icy rope of panic slipping around his neck, as she could?

His leg moved as he stomped on the gas pedal. The truck leaped forward, swerving alarmingly as he jerked the wheel again. Breath hissed through her teeth when their bumper barely cleared the rear of the car in front of them. As they sped past, she caught sight of the driver's startled expression.

The car behind followed.

"They're determined, I'll give them that." Caleb leaned forward until his chin was inches from the wheel. "Hold on."

I am holding on, she wanted to answer, but terrified lungs held her breath captive.

Their speed increased. Tall buildings on either side of the four-lane highway whipped past at dizzying speeds. She was tossed back and forth as the truck wove in and out of traffic. Horns blew as drivers trumpeted their displeasure, and still Caleb pressed forward. Beside her, Percy whimpered inside his crate.

If we crash, there's no way we'd survive. The look she gave Caleb now was fearful. He hadn't seemed like a reckless man, but only a fool would drive at these speeds in city traffic. A fool or someone who was desperate.

A sound penetrated her whirling thoughts. High, wailing. A siren. Caleb turned a satisfied smile her way.

"Who says there's never a cop around when you need one?"

Darcie twisted in the seat and looked through the rear window. A trio of police cruisers, blue lights flashing and sirens blazing, bore down on them from behind. The car that had been following slowed and was soon overtaken by a stream of cars that rushed to get over, out of the cruisers' way.

"But they're going to get away."

Caleb took his foot off the gas pedal. "Sister, the good book says there's a time for everything under heaven. Kenny Rogers sang the same thing in one of his songs. Right now's the time to walk away." He stepped on the brake as the first police car slid in behind them. "Don't worry. I have a feeling those jerks will be back."

With grim certainty, Darcie knew he was right.

* * *

The police station was full of drunks, addicts and derelicts. Caleb made a point of smiling and making eye contact with as many as he could while following the stern-faced officer through the waiting area. God's children, every one of them, even if most of them didn't know it.

The officer led them through a security door and into another room, this one smaller and less crowded. His finger stabbed toward the front row of hard plastic chairs.

"You two sit there," he barked. "I'll be back in a minute."

Caleb kept his expression pleasant. They'd already told their story to this officer, who clearly didn't know what to make of them. They'd been clocked doing ninety-five in a fifty-mile-per-hour zone. If he'd let them go, Caleb would have been surprised. No, he'd hauled them downtown so somebody higher up could be responsible for them.

He gestured for Darcie to precede him past a dozen or so rows to the front. She did, careful not to jostle the dog crate as she walked. Percy had settled down inside, thank the Lord. The high-strung pooch had not been fond of the sirens or the city traffic or, apparently, the officers who questioned them. His ceaseless high-pitched barking had set everyone's teeth on edge, even Darcie's. Only when she finally snapped, "Percy! That's enough," did the dog quiet down.

Darcie set the crate carefully on a chair before lowering herself gingerly into the one next to it, wincing. Perched on the edge, she noticed his quizzical expression.

"I landed on the ground kind of hard back at the restaurant," she explained. "I've probably got a bruise the size of Georgia on my, uh…" Pink spots appeared on her cheeks. "Rear bumper."

"Ah. I'm sorry."

Her head tilted. "It's not your fault. You saved me from much worse."

"I'm expressing sympathy, not apology." He slid onto the chair beside her. "At least my goose egg is only the side of Rhode Island."

She laughed, though the sound held no humor. He examined her face. Dark circles smudged the smooth area beneath her eyes. Her skin, creamy with a healthy glow that afternoon, was now pale. Fine blue lines showed clearly at her temples. No doubt he looked just as exhausted. What they needed was a few hours of uninterrupted sleep to clear their heads and restore their bodies.

Not gonna happen. At least not for a while.

"I hope we don't keep your friends waiting long."

Caleb had called Brent and Lauren as soon as his truck came to a stop. "I told them to go on to bed and we'll wake them up when we get there."

A nod and then she faced forward, presenting

him a view of her profile. She'd tucked her hair behind her delicate ear, all but one silky lock. His hand moved almost of its own accord to smooth it in place, but he caught himself. With a grunt, he twisted around in the chair and faced forward.

A white-faced clock hung in front of them, small enough to look like a postage stamp on the otherwise blank wall. The second hand swept its circuit around the face, but he began to wonder if the battery was low. That minute hand didn't move nearly as quickly as it should. And yet, every time he checked his watch, the clock was right on time. Periodically officers came through the door and called one of the handful of others waiting behind them, but there was no sign of the patrolman who brought them in.

At eleven-fourteen, nearly an hour after they arrived, the door finally opened and a familiar figure strode into the room.

"Detective Samuels." Dread weighed down Darcie's tone.

The man wore jeans and a white polo shirt, which gave him a far more casual look than that afternoon's business suit. His expression, however, was anything but casual. A tight-lipped scowl gave his youthful countenance a more mature, stern look. When he crossed the room and came to a stop directly in front of Darcie's chair, Caleb didn't blame her for shrinking against the molded plastic back.

"Seems you two have had a busy day." Though he spoke evenly, Caleb detected not one trace of sympathy in the man's bearing. In fact, his eyes held a hint of accusation that sent steel into Caleb's spine.

"Ms. Wiley's apartment was broken into, and then she was brutally attacked. And now the thugs are following her." Caleb folded his arms across his chest and speared one of the officers hovering behind Samuels with a glare that nearly matched the detective's. "Seems to me like somebody ought to be asking why."

Samuels's head turned toward him. "Ah, yes. Mr. Caleb Buchanan. You certainly have managed to be useful to Ms. Wiley today. Why didn't you tell me this afternoon that you're a private investigator?"

Talk about accusing. If looks could burn, Caleb would be a flaming marshmallow right about now.

"I'm not a private investigator. But I do work with one."

"Mmm-hmm." He propped an elbow on his other arm and rubbed his chin with a thumb and forefinger, watching Caleb closely. "Mr. Sinclair, I believe. And your other associate is Mr. Emerson."

That set Caleb back a second. The man had investigated F.A.S.T.

Samuels's eyes narrowed. "What I'd like to know is what you were doing on the Fairmont Estate when clearly you are not a painter by trade."

Caleb held his gaze steadily. "Exactly what I said—painting. If you've checked into my life, which you obviously have, you know that I do a lot of odd jobs. It helps pay the bills between clients."

A long moment passed during which Darcie shifted uncomfortably in her chair and Caleb fought the urge to stand up and tower over the slight detective. But why lower himself by resorting to petty intimidation tactics?

Samuels stepped around him and pulled an empty chair forward. He placed it in front of the two of them, facing backward, and straddled it. With an elbow planted on the edge and his chin resting in his hand, his gaze slid from Caleb to Darcie.

"First I'll tell you what I *think*. I think the two of you are involved in something that has an impact on my murder investigation. Whatever it is might even be the cause of the murder."

Beside Caleb, Darcie sat upright, her mouth open to speak.

Samuels stopped her with a raised finger. "Let me finish. Perhaps you've stumbled onto a situation that escalated out of control, and you had nothing to do with killing that man." His mouth hardened. "Or perhaps you killed him yourselves."

"And then we hired a pair of criminals to attack me and crack Caleb's skull with a hammer, and then we hired a couple more to chase us through the streets of Atlanta?" Darcie's eyes snapped with indignation. "That's ridiculous."

The detective silenced her with a look. "That's what I *think*. What I *know* is this." He leaned forward across the chair back. "You're neck-deep in my murder investigation. I *know* that Mrs. Fairmont, a woman of impeccable character, has some reason to dislike you even though you both claim never to have met before today. I *know* that Mr. Buchanan concealed the true nature of his employment during questioning."

If you'd asked, I would have told you. Caleb bit down on his tongue. Truthfully if he'd thought his association with F.A.S.T. had any bearing on the murder at all, he would have said something. But there was a time to defend himself and a time to keep his mouth shut.

Samuels continued, "Maybe you're both innocent, or maybe you're working together to cover something up." He caught and held Caleb's eyes in a hard stare. "Or maybe you're trying to protect someone. But hear me on this—I will not have you messing around in my murder investigation. If I suspect you are, I'll have you arrested for obstruction or some other charge that will get you out of my way. And I *will* get to the bottom of your involvement."

Know when to walk away, Caleb recited the words of the song to himself.

If continuing to argue his and Darcie's innocence would accomplish anything, he'd be up to the task. But Samuels's mind appeared to be made up. Seemed like a good time to walk away. At least until he had more evidence to back him up.

After a long and uncomfortable period during which Samuels switched his stare from one of them to the other, he finally stood.

"Go on. Get out of here. But don't leave town."

In the act of standing, Darcie cast a startled glance at the detective, but he had already turned toward the door. When he disappeared through it, his silent convoy of uniformed officers behind him, she turned to Caleb.

"Why did he say not to leave town?"

Caleb picked up the empty chair and restored it to its proper place. Then he answered grimly, "Because according to him, we're both murder suspects."

SEVEN

Darcie preceded Caleb through the doorway into the crowded police waiting room. When a group of people leaped out of chairs and rushed toward her, she skidded to a halt. If there'd been only the two men she would have screamed and fled, but there were also two women, their expressions kind.

They went to Caleb and took turns hugging him.

The blonde held him at arm's length after her hug and looked up into his face. "I'm glad you're okay. We've been praying for you."

The big man bent down to give her another hug. "Then that's why I'm okay."

The other female smiled at Darcie. Her black hair and warm brown skin spoke of Hispanic origins. "Hello. I'm Karina Sinclair. And you must be Darcie." She surprised Darcie by pulling her into a quick embrace. "We hear you've had a rough day. I'm so sorry."

"Thank you." To her utter embarrassment, tears prickled in Darcie's eyes. Detective Samuels's harsh accusations and insinuations frightened and angered her, but the kind words of a stranger reduced her to tears. *I'm an emotional mess tonight.*

Karina kindly pretended not to notice and nodded toward the blonde. "This is Lauren, and these are our husbands, Mason and Brent."

With some focused swallowing and blinking of eyelids, Darcie got herself under control enough to offer a quick smile. Lauren was the name Caleb had mentioned, the one who had agreed to shelter her and Percy for a day or two.

Caleb looked around the group. "What are you doing here? I told you to go on to bed."

Mason splayed out his hands. "Dude, do you really think we're gonna let our friend sit in the hoosegow without his buddies?"

Brent's lips twisted. "We met your new friend, Detective Samuels."

Mason whistled a low tone. "That is one uptight cop."

If she weren't so tired, Darcie would have laughed. Uptight? Well, that was one way to describe the man.

"Ah, that explains how he knew about F.A.S.T." Caleb sounded relieved. "I thought he'd been investigating me."

"Well, I wouldn't get too comfortable in thinking you're off the hook," Brent said. "He seemed pretty irritated to find out about our investigative work."

Mason clapped Caleb on the shoulder. "Don't worry, buddy. We'll get to the bottom of this."

Percy's crate seemed to pick up an extra ten

pounds when a wave of exhaustion washed over Darcie. She wavered on her feet.

Lauren was beside her in an instant. "Here, let me take that. You're worn out. Let's get you home."

Relieved, Darcie relinquished the crate. With an effort she placed one foot in front of the other to follow the women out of the station, the men trailing behind.

At the direction of the police, they'd pulled Caleb's truck into a parking lot before being brought to the station. The officer at the front desk confirmed that the pickup had not been impounded. Karina and Mason promised to come to the Emersons' in the morning, then climbed into their car while Darcie followed Lauren and Brent to a silver Lexus. She slid into the backseat and scooted across to make room for Caleb. Percy's crate was once again stationed between them. Caleb gave Brent directions to the location of the truck, and the Lexus followed the Sinclairs' car out of the police station's parking lot.

A comfortable silence filled the car's interior. So comfortable, in fact, that Darcie's eyelids grew heavy. It would be embarrassing to fall asleep in these people's car, so she cleared her throat and broke the silence.

"Thank you for letting Percy and me stay with you. I really appreciate it."

Lauren half turned in the passenger seat. "We're glad to have you. I've been in a similar situation, so

I know how hard it is to feel like you have nowhere safe to go."

"You have?"

Green light from the instrument panel reflected off honey-blond hair as Lauren turned a smile on her husband. "That's how we met."

Caleb provided the explanation. "Lauren was falsely accused of killing someone, and Brent helped her get out of it."

"Not just me," Brent corrected. "Things would have turned out a lot different without you and Mason."

"That's how the Falsely Accused Support Team got started," Caleb said. "We worked together to find the real killer. Brent's a whiz with a computer, and Mason's uncanny at investigation work."

Lauren twisted farther to raise an eyebrow in his direction. "I helped out a little, too, don't forget."

A genuine laugh filled the car. "Yes, you did, sister." He turned a grin toward Darcie. "I hope you're a better houseguest than Lauren was. When she stayed with me, she set my house on fire."

"Only your back porch." Lauren's protest was delivered with a companionable smile. "And saved your hide in the process, *brother*."

"That you did."

Their companionable banter spoke of shared troubles and deep friendship. Darcie felt more of her tension seep away.

Curious, she looked at Caleb. "What's your role in the team?"

He shrugged. "They let me hang around because they feel sorry for me."

"Not true." Brent grinned into the rearview mirror. "I don't feel sorry for you one bit, you big ox."

"Caleb is our 'ear to the street,'" Lauren told her. "Everybody knows him and trusts him. so they talk to him. He digs up tips that no one else could get."

He held up a finger to clarify. "Addicts, gangsters and generally disreputable people trust me. They'll tell me things they won't tell a cop or a private investigator." He flexed the muscles in the arm closest to Darcy. "But mostly my friends use me as their bodyguard. That's about all I'm good for."

"Not true, Preacher Man." Lauren bestowed an affectionate glance on him before telling Darcie, "His most important contribution is providing spiritual guidance and prayer cover."

Darcie looked at Caleb with new interest. Preacher Man? Somehow she didn't have to stretch her imagination very far to see him giving guidance, and she'd already seen him pray.

"So you can see that you're in good hands, Darcie," said Lauren. "These guys will get to the bottom of everything."

Darcie's gaze slid from her to the back of Brent's head and finally to Caleb. Maybe they really could help her. Maybe the life she had hoped to start in Atlanta wasn't completely wrecked after all.

No. I can't stay here.

She shook off the feeling of false hope. Coming to Atlanta had been a mistake. Calling Mr. Fairmont for help had been an even bigger one. There was only one thing she could do. Leave.

"I appreciate your help. I really do." She included Lauren and Brent both in her glance. "But I think the best thing I can do is put this all behind me and start over." She looked at Caleb. "As soon as I can, I'm leaving Georgia."

A curious guilt wrenched her heart at the look of utter betrayal on his face.

Darcie's words fell on Caleb like blows. His instincts had been right all along. She was just like Anita.

"That's the most immature decision I've ever heard." The words snapped out before he could stop them.

Her expression became incredulous. "Pardon me?"

"You heard me. Let me spell it out for you. Leaving town is the stupidest thing you could do."

Part of his brain urged caution. But the other part was reeling from the realization that he'd been duped again. He'd let his desire to rescue a soul in trouble overcome good sense.

Her incredulity gave way to anger. She glared darts across the top of the dog crate. "Did you call me stupid?"

From the front seat Lauren said, "I'm sure he

didn't mean——" At a sharp glance from her husband she fell silent and turned around in her seat.

"You heard the detective." Caleb ground the words between his teeth before releasing them. "He told us both not to leave town."

Spine ramrod straight, she snapped, "Maybe you didn't hear me say *as soon as I can*. I'm not *stupid* enough to run away from the police. But I'm also not stupid enough to stick around and let myself be attacked again. Next time I might not be so lucky."

Luck didn't save you. I did. That time he managed to bite his tongue. Thankfully, Brent pulled the car into the parking lot at that moment. Caleb's pickup was parked exactly where he had left it.

He opened his door before the Lexus came to a full stop. He couldn't get out of that car fast enough.

"Pop the trunk." His voice sounded brusque, the words clipped, so he added, "Please. I'll get her stuff out of the pickup."

Lauren turned in surprise. "You're not coming home with us?"

"What for?" A snort escaped. "She'll be fine with you two. She doesn't need me."

His gaze slid for one moment to Darcie's face, which was flushed with anger. Then he shut the door. When her things were transferred, he slammed the trunk of the Lexus with a little more force than necessary. Then he climbed into his truck, started the engine and pulled out of the parking space without another glance her way. He did lift a hand in thanks and farewell to Brent as he rolled from the parking lot onto the main road.

Finally, when the wheels of his truck were rolling smoothly down the road, putting distance between him and Darcie, his head began to clear.

What's the matter with me? I'm acting like an idiot. If she wants to leave Atlanta when this is over, let her. No skin off my nose.

But his attempt at self-pep talk didn't work. He *knew* what was wrong. He'd flown off the handle not because of Darcie's decision to leave Atlanta, but because that decision reminded him so starkly and painfully of Anita.

Which meant he'd unconsciously developed deeper feelings than mere friendship for Darcie.

"I told You this would happen." The angry words were slung heavenward. "I knew this woman was prone to run, just like Anita. I told You I didn't want to get involved."

He did not speak the question that dragged at his heart like a truckload of cement. *Why are You doing this to me again? Are You trying to hurt me?* To pour out his hurts to God was one thing. To accuse the Almighty of cruelty aloud bordered on blasphemy.

One thing was certain. His involvement with Darcie stopped here.

Only...I promised to help her.

His grip on the steering wheel tightened. No, he hadn't. He had promised that F.A.S.T. would help her. And they would. She was in good hands with Brent and Mason.

I can't pawn her off on my friends and then stand by and do nothing. I'm not that guy. If only I'd never made that promise. If only I'd never felt that nudge.

Had the Lord urged him to help Darcie? Or had that been his imagination, his budding attraction for her overpowering his ability to listen to the spiritual voice that had guided him in the past?

Doubt spilled over him like dirt on a coffin. If he'd mistaken God's voice for his own this time, it would happen again.

A void seemed to gather around him, and Caleb felt utterly alone.

An hour later Caleb's angry words still rang in Darcie's ears. She and Percy sat in an armchair in the corner of Lauren's guest room. After a few wild circuits to investigate his new surroundings, the little dog had settled down in her lap, content to let her pet him. He didn't even seem to mind the tear or two that dripped off her chin and disappeared in his fur.

The exhaustion that had weighed her down earlier had deserted her, chased away by a whirlwind of worries and fears—and questions.

Why did he get so angry with me?

The question went unanswered, but pondering it had made her aware of one thing. Caleb was right. Though oh so tempting, running away from a stalker who had already followed her once was a stupid idea. If she didn't find out now why she was being targeted, she would live in fear and uncertainty no matter where she went. She didn't want that. What she wanted was peace.

A quiet knock sounded on the bedroom door.

With a sniff and a quick swab at her wet cheeks, she said, "Come in."

The door opened and Lauren stepped inside. "I saw your light on so I knew you were awake. Are you comfortable in here? Anything I can get you?"

"Everything is wonderful. It's a beautiful room." She glanced around at the tasteful decorations. A real oil painting graced the wall above the gleaming cherry dresser. Above the matching dressing table hung a mirror in an ornately gilded frame. The carved posters at each corner of the bed stood taller than Darcie. "I really do appreciate you and Brent letting us stay."

Lauren waved a hand in dismissal as she crossed the room and perched on the edge of the mattress facing Darcie. "We're glad to have you." She grinned at the sleeping dog. "Percy, too. He sure is adorable."

As though aware that he was being discussed, Percy raised his head, opened a sleepy eye to look at Lauren and then settled back into Darcie's lap with a sigh.

After a short silence, Lauren went on, "I do know some of what you're going through. If you need an ear to listen, I'm here."

"Thank you." Darcie smiled at a sudden memory. "Did you really set Caleb's house on fire?"

"I sure did."

They shared a quiet laugh.

"Speaking of Caleb." Darcie cleared her throat, aware that this woman was Caleb's friend. "What did I say to upset him?"

"I don't know." She shook her head, clearly perplexed. "I've never seen him flare up like that. He's always so calm and levelheaded. The first one to pray, too." She peered into Darcie's eyes. "Are you a believer?"

Darcie averted her eyes. "I used to be." That was a topic she didn't want to discuss right now. She had too much hanging over her head to worry about a God who had either forgotten she existed or didn't care about her troubles.

As though she sensed Darcie's hesitancy, Lauren changed the subject. "I sent everyone a text and told them to come for breakfast at ten o'clock tomorrow. Brent has an early meeting at work. He's a vice president at Sterling Foods, so he can't really miss this meeting, but is going to try to get home by then. Karina answered that they'd be here." She rose. "Get some sleep. And don't worry. F.A.S.T. is good. They'll find a way out of this mess."

Darcie's fingers ran through Percy's soft fur, and she asked in a carefully casual voice, "Will Caleb be here, too?"

An upward glance showed her that she'd failed in

her attempt at nonchalance. A smile hovered around Lauren's lips. "I'm sure he will. Caleb never misses an invitation to a meal." She paused in the act of turning toward the door, her expression serious. "And he can always be counted on to help someone in need. Always."

With a final good-night she left the room. The door closed with a soft click.

Alone with her thoughts, Darcie continued to stroke Percy. Was Lauren right? Would F.A.S.T. find out what was at the bottom of these attempts to kidnap or hurt her? She wanted to believe it, wanted it badly. Maybe it was time to trust someone else for a change.

Who am I kidding? I have to trust them. Where else will I go?

A sense of helplessness stole over her. She had no other option. Tomorrow over breakfast she would force herself to open up to these people. She'd lay it all out for them. Hold nothing back. If they were as good as Lauren claimed, they might be able to piece something together that she had missed.

And what of Caleb?

An emotion she refused to name stabbed at her. "He can always be counted on to help someone in need." There had been no hesitation, no doubt in Lauren's tone when she said that.

Oh, if only I could believe her.

She wanted to believe in Caleb, to trust him. But even thinking of his name probed at a tender place in her heart, a place she shied away from. Placing her trust in the one they called Preacher Man was more frightening than being stalked by kidnappers.

EIGHT

Karina and Mason arrived a little before ten while Darcie was mixing up a pitcher of frozen orange juice.

"Good morning." Mason's booming voice preceded him through the arched doorway into the kitchen. He raised his nose and inhaled loudly. "Mmmm. Are those cinnamon rolls I smell?"

Grinning, Lauren turned from her task of drizzling icing over a pan of piping hot rolls. "Of course. I know they're your favorite."

Karina planted her hands on her hips and fixed a mock-stern stare on him. "You can only have two. This time you're going to share with everyone else."

Percy charged into the kitchen, yapping wildly at the arrival of new people. He'd spent the morning investigating the house and apparently had decided it was his territory to protect.

A delighted squeal rose from Karina, and she bent down to look at him. "Oh my goodness! He is the cutest puppy I've ever seen. Hi, fella." She stretched out a hand, and Percy stopped barking to sniff it.

"Isn't he? I've had so much fun playing with him this morning." Lauren scraped the last of the icing out of the measuring cup. "Darcie, would you put these on the table please? I need to check on those burritos."

Darcie picked up the baking dish full of fragrant cinnamon rolls and set it on the table. She stretched her neck to look through the doorway and down the hall. "I thought Caleb would be here by now." A nearly imperceptible knot of worry wiggled its way into her voice.

"He lives in the other direction," Mason said over his shoulder as he hovered over the table. He stuck a finger into the warm icing and put it in his mouth. "I'm sure he'll be here in a minute."

The sound of the front door opening came from the hallway, and Percy charged out of the room, barking like a fiend. Darcie's breath caught in her chest. Was it Caleb?

"Here now, what's all the ruckus?"

At the sound of Brent's voice, her breath deflated. The ornate clock on the wall read 10:05 a.m. Caleb's anger last night lay heavy on her, though she didn't care to think about why it should. All she knew was that her tension mounted with every minute that passed. What if he didn't come?

Brent appeared, Percy dancing back and forth at his feet and barking furiously. A chuckle lightened his words. "I feel like I've been attacked by a fearsome butterfly."

When everyone laughed, Percy apparently decided this stranger was safe and stopped barking. He trotted over to sit at Darcie's feet and look up at her, tail wagging, as though to say, "See, Mom? I'm protecting you."

"Breakfast is almost ready," Lauren announced, pulling a huge tray of breakfast burritos from the oven. "Darcie, the juice glasses are in that cabinet behind you."

Glad for a task to keep her hands busy, Darcie swallowed her rising worry and opened the cabinet.

The front door opened again, and Percy rushed to do his duty. Was Caleb finally here? Darcie's heart thudded in her chest. She forced herself to remove six glasses from the cabinet, even though some strange part of her wanted to run after Percy. Was Caleb still upset with her?

Anger sparked at the thought. What was the matter with her? What did she care? He had no reason to be angry. She didn't call *him* stupid, after all.

Percy fell silent in the hallway. Tiny claws clicked on the tile, triple time to the sound of heavy footsteps.

"Hey, dude, you're just in time." Mason scooted a chair out and dropped into it. "We were getting ready to start without you."

"Sorry. Ran into traffic."

Darcie set the last glass in place before turning to look at him. When she did, she found Caleb's eyes fixed on her.

"Good morning. Did you get any sleep?" His tone was guarded, his eyes politely distant.

"I slept well," she replied in an equally polite voice. "Did you?"

"Yes, a little." His weight shifted from one foot to another. "I want to apologize for last night." His glance included Brent and Lauren. "I was tired, I guess, but I shouldn't have lost my temper. I'm sorry."

The apology appeared to be genuine, but Darcie found herself disappointed at the impersonal tone in which it was delivered. She managed a nod, then turned away to retrieve the juice pitcher from the counter. That was it? A quick "I'm sorry," and he expected everything to be forgiven? On the other hand, what did she expect? Groveling?

"We were all tired," Brent said.

"I know I was." Lauren, her hands still swathed in oven mitts, gave Darcie a quick, expectant look.

Oh, okay. Her attention focused on pouring a steady stream of juice into the first glass. "We had a long, stressful day yesterday. I'm sorry I lost my temper, too."

Karina and Mason were watching all of them, their expressions curious. Mason opened his mouth to speak, and a muted sound thud came from beneath the table.

"Ow!" He looked at his wife reproachfully. "I was only going to say now that we have that out of the way, it's time to eat."

Lauren laughed and asked Karina good-naturedly, "Don't you feed him at home?"

That lightened the atmosphere, and they all slid into chairs, obviously comfortable with their positions. Darcie took the empty one next to Caleb. Percy lay obediently on the floor between them.

Brent looked at Caleb. "Would you pray for us?"

Caleb made a show of unfolding his napkin and laying it across his lap. "I'd rather you lead us, brother."

A long, silent pause fell on those seated at the table. Several jaws slackened, and everyone stared at the one they called Preacher Man. Darcie stole a sideways glance. Caleb's lips were pressed into a tight line, his stare fixed on his plate as though examining it for spots. What was it Lauren said last night? He was the first one to pray. Which meant something was bothering him today, something that made him not want to offer the blessing. The thought disturbed her. She might not have the Lord's attention, but it was comforting to know people like Caleb who did. The idea that he might have a few doubts, as she did, was distinctly unsettling.

Brent recovered himself. "Uh, sure. Let's pray."

He extended his hand and Darcie, startled, stared at it for a moment. Then she saw that everyone else had joined hands. Feeling shy, she slipped her left hand into his. On her right, Caleb hesitated. Heat crept up her neck from her collarbone. Did he not want to hold her hand?

He lifted his hands from his lap and grabbed hers and Lauren's. His felt hot and clammy, and it engulfed hers.

"Lord, we're grateful to be here with each other and with You. Thank You for drawing us together as friends. We're especially grateful for our new friend, Darcie. We ask You to keep her safe. Direct our conversation this morning as we figure out how to help her." Brent's hand squeezed hers, and a flush warmed Darcie's cheeks, but she kept her eyes tightly shut. "Bless this delicious food and the lovely hands that have prepared it for us. In Christ's name, Amen."

Caleb released her hand quickly. The prickle of tears came unexpectedly. Why? Was it because Brent's heartfelt words reminded her of Mama's prayers, always grateful even up to the end? Or because the warmth of being named as a friend was chilled by Caleb's eagerness to escape her touch? She lifted her juice glass to hide her effort to get her emotions under control. Apparently a good night's sleep had not restored her as much as she had thought.

"Oh, yum." Across the table, Mason's face took on a rapturous expression as he bit into a warm roll. "Awesome, Mrs. Emerson. Awesome."

A dimple creased Lauren's cheek. "Thank you, Mr. Sinclair."

The rolls were delicious, as was the burrito stuffed with eggs, chorizo, onions and peppers. Small talk dwindled as everyone enjoyed the breakfast. Darcie ate silently, content to let the conversation ebb and flow around her. The obvious affection these people had for each other made her a little envious. Had she ever had someone who cared about her the way they cared about each other? Besides Mama, anyway. Not really. Oh, she'd had girlfriends in school, but they'd all drifted away when Mama got sick. No, if she was honest with herself, she'd withdrawn from them, let the relationships grow cold. She was too preoccupied taking care of Mama to return their calls.

She stole a glance at Caleb. He, too, sat silent, his attention on his plate. The space between them felt like an invisible wall. Where had the friendly, caring man of yesterday gone?

When Brent's plate was empty, he pushed it away and picked up his glass. "I have to go back to work this afternoon, so I think it's time we get down to business."

Though half a burrito still lay on her plate, Darcie's appetite disappeared. She set her fork on the rim of her plate. Discomfort congealed in her stomach along with the good food, leaving her slightly sick. The time had come. If she wanted these people to help her, she had to open the pages of her past for them to see.

With a glance at Karina, Mason lifted a third cinnamon roll out of the pan. "Let's start with yesterday. Tell us exactly what happened."

Darcie was still gathering her thoughts when Caleb spoke. "It started with a murder."

She listened as he succinctly laid everything out, from their initial meeting beside the pool house to their discovery of Jason Lewis's body, to the interrogation on the Fairmont's patio. He summarized the conversation with Detective Samuels and Mrs. Fairmont's appearance. As she listened, Darcie once again felt the hot misery of the woman's disdainful gaze, the horror of the attacker's hand clamping over her mouth, the terror of the race through crowded city streets. When he finished, she drooped against the seat back, exhausted.

The rest listened attentively, and only when Caleb fell silent did Brent speak. "I don't understand Samuels's suspicions. There's not a single piece of evidence regarding that murder pointing to Darcie."

"I know, right?" Mason wiped his fingers with his napkin. "She's a victim. Anybody can see that."

"I think it's because Mrs. Fairmont and that housekeeper, Mrs. Byler, dislike her." Karina directed a sympathetic smile across the table.

Lauren rose and went after the juice pitcher. "What's that all about anyway? Did you do something to offend her, Darcie?"

"*I* didn't. But my mother might have."

"Not your uncle?" asked Brent.

"Well, both of them." She looked at Caleb, who nodded and slid his chair back.

"I'll get the box. It's in the truck."

While he was gone, Lauren refilled glasses and

Brent began stacking the empty plates. Caleb returned, with Percy trotting at his heels, and set the shoe box on the table in front of her.

Moisture dampened her palms as she lifted the lid. Everything in there reminded her of Mama. The faint smell of the lilac hand lotion she liked rose from inside. Darcie's fingers trembled as she pushed aside the trinkets her mother had stored there. A small, misshapen clay dish Darcie had made for her in fourth grade. A miniature spiral notebook, each page decorated with colored hearts and flowers and a silly story scrawled in slanting, uneven letters. A medal Darcie had won at 4-H camp. The gaudy collar that had been delivered with Percy, which they'd never forced him to wear, along with his AKC papers. From beneath those things she withdrew a stack of papers held together by a rubber band and put the lid back on the box.

"I found these when I was getting ready to move to Atlanta."

There were no envelopes, only a dozen or so single sheets of paper. She unfolded the first and examined the even script that sprawled across the page.

Per our agreement.
Richard Fairmont

Wordlessly, she handed it to Caleb, who read it and passed it to Lauren.

The first was the only note that bore a signature. The rest included only a single line, though in the same handwriting. She picked a sample few. One read:

As promised.

Another:

I trust you are both well.

And the one that had caused her heart to skip when she'd first read it:

She looks like you, thank goodness.

When that one circled the table to Karina, she studied it, her expression thoughtful. "A shame there are no dates on any of these."

"I know." A sentimental expression softened Lauren's features. "There might be a tragic love story behind these notes. A love that could never be. Did your mother ever mention Richard Fairmont?"

"Not that way," Darcie said. "In fact, I never even heard his name until I was eleven or twelve, when Uncle Kenneth went to work for him."

"Ah, yes. Uncle Kenneth." Mason folded his arms on the table and leaned over them. "Tell us about him."

Shame fell over her like hot rain. She had a hard time meeting anyone's eye and fixed her gaze instead on the empty glass in front of her. "Uncle Kenneth is Mama's younger brother. When I was little he used to come around a lot. I didn't like him. He was…mean."

"Mean?" Caleb turned in his chair to look at her head-on, his expression fierce. "Did he hurt you?"

"Only once. Most of the time he hardly even looked at me. But he made fun of my mother, called her stupid and…" Heat burned in her face. "And a tramp. She loved him, but he upset her every time he came over."

"The poor woman." Softhearted Lauren sounded like she might cry.

Darcie managed a grateful smile. "She used to give him money and he would disappear for a while, but he always came back. When I was young I told Mama I didn't like him, but she said he was her little brother and our only relation, so we had to make an effort to get along with him.

"One day I came home from school and his car was in the driveway. I tiptoed into the house, planning to slip into my room without him seeing me. He and Mama were in the kitchen, arguing. Well, he was arguing. Shouting. Mama was crying. I heard him say something about somebody owing Mama, and she was stupid for not cashing in on it. She told him she wouldn't do it, that Richard Fairmont had helped enough."

"Fairmont had helped enough," Caleb repeated thoughtfully.

Darcie squeezed her eyes shut. Mama's sobs still echoed in her ears, and her stomach clenched into the same painful knot it had ten years ago. She found that she had picked up her table knife and held it clenched in her right hand. With an effort, she laid it gently on the tablecloth.

"That was the first time I heard Mr. Fairmont's name. Shortly after that, Mama told me that Uncle Kenneth had gotten a job in Atlanta and was moving. He was going to work for a man named Mr. Fairmont. Even at that age I knew what had happened."

"Your uncle knew of your mother's relationship with Fairmont and forced her to use her influence to get him a job," Brent stated the fact plainly.

Darcie nodded. "All I cared about was that my uncle was moving away, and we wouldn't see him much anymore. I didn't hear Mr. Fairmont's name again for four years, when Uncle Kenneth came back."

Karina leaned forward. "You were how old then? Seventeen?"

"That's right. We were washing up the supper dishes and he banged on the back door. When Mama let him in, he ran around the house closing all the blinds. Mama told me to go to my room so they could talk."

Darcie closed her eyes again, the scene as vivid as if it had happened yesterday. She could still hear the harsh bitterness in Uncle Kenneth's voice.

"Let her stay," he said. "She might as well know the truth."

Mama paled. "Kenneth, don't."

His bark of laughter filled the room. "Don't worry. I'll keep your trashy little secret. I mean the truth about the high-and-mighty Richard Fairmont. He's nothing but a petty crook."

Mama's back stiffened. "He is not."

Surprised, Darcie looked at her. Mama never disagreed with her brother, especially in such an angry voice.

"You don't know him like I do. That man's as crooked as a corkscrew." He paced to the front window and parted the curtains with a finger to peek out. "He's after me. He caught me with my fingers in his pie and he told me if I don't take the rap quietly, he'd hurt you."

"I don't believe that." Mama's chin jutted into the air.

Darcie could hardly believe her ears. She rounded on her uncle. "He said he'd hurt your sister, and you ran away? You're hiding behind a woman? You're nothing but a coward."

Eyes blazing, he stomped across the floor toward her. "Shut up." He pulled back a hand and before she could react, sharp pain exploded in her cheek.

The memory of the slap still produced a vivid stinging pain five years later. Darcie rubbed a finger lightly over her cheek, and then dropped her hand into her lap when she realized everyone was staring at her.

A humorless attempt at a laugh sounded pathetic in the silence around the table. "I'd never spoken up to him before then, which is probably a good thing."

Mason cleared his throat. "He sounds like a real sweetheart. What happened to him?"

Darcie toyed with her spoon and attempted nonchalance. "Oh, he stayed for a couple of hours, ranting and raving the whole time about how Richard Fairmont was a crook, but he knew he'd come out on top in the end. And then the police came and arrested him."

"At your house?" Caleb asked.

"That's right." She balanced the spoon between her thumb and forefinger. "They handcuffed him in our living room. All the neighbors came outside and watched as they put him in the police car."

Chair legs scraped across tile as Lauren stood. She rounded the table to place an arm around Darcie's shoulders and squeeze. "You poor thing. That must have been so traumatic."

Darcie shrugged. "Mama took it harder than me. I was glad to see him go."

Mason drained his orange juice and set the glass on the table. "So Mrs. Fairmont has a couple of grudges against you."

Karina stiffened, her expression outraged. "That's not fair. Darcie isn't responsible for her uncle's actions, or her mother's either."

Her defense touched a soft place in Darcie's heart, and she smiled wordless thanks across the table.

"Even so," said Brent, "I agree with Caleb that Samuels's main reason to suspect Darcie is Mrs. Fairmont's dislike of her, regardless of the reason. And the housekeeper is probably siding with her employer."

Caleb had mostly remained silent while she talked. Now he stirred. "It's clear to me what the next steps are. Do you agree?"

His question was directed at Mason and Brent. They both nodded, their expressions serious.

"What?" she asked. "What's the next step?"

"We need to talk to your uncle." He leaned back in the chair and folded his arms across his chest. "And you need to confront Fairmont."

Dread descended over her like icy waters over a drowning victim.

NINE

Caleb saw Darcie go pale. She had told him last night she'd considered confronting Fairmont about his relationship with her mother and rejected the idea. He knew she wouldn't want to do this, but he didn't see any way around it.

"No." She shook her head. "I don't want to see either of them."

Though he understood her reluctance and felt sympathy for all she'd been through, she was being unreasonable. How could he keep her safe if she wouldn't cooperate? He fought against the irritation that made him want to snap hasty words and spoke in a carefully calm voice.

"If last night's kidnapping attempt is related to Lewis's murder, we need to figure out how. To do that we look for connections."

On the other side of Darcie, Brent leaned forward. "The only visible connection between the murder and you is Fairmont. The reason you found the body was because you were on his property, and the reason you were on his property is because he gave you a job, just like he gave your uncle a job."

Mason nodded agreement. "Maybe five years in the slammer has improved your slimy uncle's outlook and he can tell us something helpful about Fairmont."

"I doubt that," Darcie said bitterly.

Lauren returned to the table after carrying a stack of dirty plates to the counter. "Besides, if Mr. Fairmont is your father maybe he'll help us figure out who's trying to harm you."

A gloomy thought occurred to Caleb, but before he could speak it, Darcie did.

"Unless he's the one responsible." Her gaze sought his. "What if Uncle Kenneth was right and he's a crook?"

The stark fear in her eyes plucked a protective chord in him. "He won't hurt you. I'll make sure of that."

"Where's your uncle in prison?" asked Brent.

She raised her hands to her forehead and pressed her temples. "Uh, Hancock State Prison. I don't know where that is, though."

"It's in Sparta, a couple of hours away." At her raised eyebrow, Caleb shrugged. "I know these things. I used to be a guard at the Atlanta Detention Center."

"We can make a call this morning and find out if she's listed as a family member on his visitor list," Mason said.

Caleb nodded. She stood the best chance of getting the man to talk. No way he was letting Darcie visit with that jerk alone, though. "I'm going with her. I'll apply for a special visitor permit. Got a buddy down there, and maybe he can pull a few strings."

She shot him a quick, grateful glance.

"That'll take a few days," Mason said. "We'd better get the ball rolling this morning."

"And didn't you say that Mr. Fairmont was out of town?" asked Karina.

Darcie nodded, relief obvious on her features. "Mrs. Byler said he was in Washington, DC. I don't know when he'll be back."

Brent leaned back. "Well, looks like we're at a standstill for now."

The idea of hanging around for a few days doing nothing didn't sit right with Caleb. They had to do something. But what? Then he remembered something he'd mentioned to Darcie before.

He looked at Mason. "You got plans today, brother?"

"A couple of subpoenas to serve and some paperwork." Mason shook his head. "Nothing that can't wait. What's up?"

"I want you to take a look at her apartment. See if you can find any signs of an intruder."

"All right then." Brent slapped his hands on the table. "We don't have much to go on, but at least we have a plan."

Lauren smiled at Darcie. "You and Percy can hang

out here. It'll do you good to relax for a few days after what you've been through."

A kind offer, but the troubled look on Darcie's face did not fade. She shook her head.

"I can't sit here and do nothing." She looked at Mason and then him. "I'm going with you."

His stomach twisted at her words, but he didn't argue. Though he was reluctant to spend any more time with her than necessary, he'd promised to keep her safe. Promised it twice, in fact. He couldn't do that from a distance.

Mutely, he nodded.

Caleb directed Mason to a parking place near Darcie's building. When he shut off the engine, the three of them emerged from his car.

"That's mine." Darcie pointed out her apartment.

While the two of them headed toward the door, Caleb stood in place, turning slowly in a three-sixty to examine the area. It had been dark last night but now he could see. This was a nice place. The people who managed this complex paid attention to the grounds. The buildings were all in good condition, not a sign of peeling paint anywhere. The grass lining the sidewalk was neatly trimmed. Big, bushy shrubs bordered the buildings, deep green and healthy looking. Shrubs that size could easily hide a man.

He joined Darcie, who stood on the sidewalk in

front of her apartment, watching Mason inspect the doorknob.

"See anything?" he asked.

"Nope." Mason turned to look at Darcie. "Is this the only entrance?"

She shook her head. "There are sliding glass doors going out to a patio on the back. But I keep those latched and a baseball bat wedged in the tracks."

"That's good, but you really need a dead bolt on this door. Watch this."

From his pocket he pulled a pair of needle-nose pliers and a couple of paper clips. He held them up. "Standard paper clips. You can get them anywhere."

He straightened them both and then, using the pliers, twisted a hook at the end of one. He knelt before the door and stuck the crooked end into the lock. Holding that in place, he inserted the straight end of the other clip. He jiggled it for a moment and gave a quick twist. The lock opened with an audible *click*.

"*Voilà.*" Mason straightened and, with a flourish, opened Darcie's door.

She stood with her mouth gaping. Caleb cocked his head to spear his friend with a suspicious look. "Where'd you learn how to do that?"

Mason's expression became sardonic. "YouTube, where any petty thief with access to the internet can see a video demonstration."

"Or any kidnapper." A shudder rippled through Darcie's body.

Unbelievable. Caleb set his jaw. "We're installing a dead bolt before you come back here."

Looking faintly sick, she nodded.

He followed Mason and Darcie into the apartment. A quick glance around showed everything exactly the same as when they'd left last night.

Mason checked the patio door and pronounced it secure. As Caleb had observed when he inspected the place, the windows had locks that could be popped from outside but not without breaking them and leaving evidence of forced entry. None showed evidence of tampering. The only sign at all that anyone had been in the apartment was the edge of the quilt hanging out of the box, and they had only Darcie's word that it had been moved.

"Sorry." Mason shrugged. "Wish I could have found something that would make the cops sit up and take notice."

Disappointed, Caleb clapped him on the shoulder. "It's all right. You tried."

They locked the door when they left, though Caleb realized what a flimsy safeguard that was. They headed for Mason's car.

Darcie stopped. "Wait. If my car's going to be here for a few days, I want to get the title and registration out of the glove box."

"Good idea," Caleb told her.

They stood on the sidewalk while she pulled her keys out of her purse. During the few short steps to her car, she punched the unlock button. When she got to the passenger side, instead of opening the door she stood staring down at it. The stillness that crept over her body set off alarms in Caleb's brain.

"What's wrong?" He hastened after her.

She fixed wide eyes on him and pointed.

The metal on the passenger door was wrinkled and bent. It had been jimmied open.

Darcie sat on the concrete step in front of her apartment, her elbows on her knees and chin in her hands. She watched Caleb and Mason inspect the damage to her car while they waited for the police to arrive. Though the break-in had come as a surprise, she wasn't nearly as alarmed as she should be. Too many shocks in the past twenty-four hours had numbed her.

A police cruiser turned into the lot, and she straightened to get a look at it. Their experience with the police recently had left her hesitant to involve them. Instead of calling 911, Caleb had called an acquaintance on the force. That morning he'd said only addicts and derelicts trusted him, but it seemed he had friends on both sides of the law.

The cruiser slowed when it entered the lot, and Caleb walked out into the open to wave it down. She hefted herself off the step and joined him as the car glided to a stop. A uniformed officer around Caleb's age got out.

"Hey, Buchanan, long time." Their hands slapped together in an enthusiastic greeting.

"Too long," Caleb answered. "Thanks for coming. I was praying you'd be on duty."

"Even if I wasn't, all you've got to do is call." His gaze slid from Caleb to Darcie. "Hello. I'm Jarron Roberts."

Jarron was one of those fresh-faced police officers whose military-style haircut made him appear younger than he was. Intelligence gleamed in the eyes he fixed on her, eyes she doubted missed much.

Caleb did the introduction. "This is Darcie Wiley and that's Mason Sinclair. They're friends."

Darcie forced herself to smile at Jarron instead of searching Caleb's face. Did he consider her a friend? Today he'd been polite and kind, but his easy manner of yesterday had not returned.

When Jarron had shaken their hands, he jerked a nod at her car. "Is this the one?"

"Yeah." Caleb led the way to the passenger side. "Looks like they used a crowbar to me."

The officer cocked his head, staring at the damage. "Me, too. Note the scratches on the edges. That was done by metal." He looked up at Darcie. "What'd they get?"

"I haven't looked."

"We didn't want to touch anything until you'd seen it," Caleb explained.

"Good idea. Let's see if we can lift any prints."

He went to his cruiser and returned with a hard gray case. Darcie watched him apply black powder with a soft brush and then gently blow the residue away. She stood back while all three men bent to study the result.

Caleb's shoulders slumped when he stood. "Nothing."

"We might find something inside." Jarron didn't sound hopeful.

"I'll be surprised if we do," Mason said. "Somebody who's prepared enough to pick a door lock would take precautions against leaving fingerprints."

Jarron pulled out a blue rubber glove and handed it to Darcie. "Take a look and let me know what's missing."

The glove was much too big for her hand, but that didn't matter. She opened the driver door and slid into the seat. The stereo was intact. She opened the ashtray. The loose coins she always tossed in there had not been disturbed. In the glove compartment she found the owner's manual, registration, proof of insurance and the various receipts for oil changes she kept there.

Caleb called from behind the car, "Pop the trunk."

She did, and she was not surprised when he said, "Nothing missing here."

So the thief had broken into her car but taken nothing. Same as her apartment. More confused than ever, she got out and joined the men standing behind the trunk.

"I can file a vandalism report," Jarron told her. "That way your insurance company will cover the damage. I don't know what else I can do, though."

Frustration knotted her stomach. "I'm being followed and someone attacked me. Why won't the police do anything?" Tears choked her words, but she didn't care.

His expression softened. "I'll pull all the reports filed yesterday and add mine to it. Then I'll go talk to my sergeant. He's a good man."

"Will you talk to Detective Samuels, too?" Caleb asked.

Jarron actually winced. "I think I'll leave that to my sergeant. His opinion will carry more weight than mine."

Caleb heaved a sigh and clapped Jarron on the shoulder. "Thanks, brother. Whatever you can do, we appreciate it."

"Give me a minute to get that report written." He started toward his cruiser, but he stopped when he drew abreast of Darcie. "My advice to you is to stick close to him." He jerked his head toward Caleb. "He's one of the best. I'd trust him with *my* life."

She managed a nod and a shaky smile.

Mason straightened from his position leaning against the trunk of her car. "I've got a buddy who does auto body work. He's good and he's cheap. Want me to give him a call and see if he has time to look at your door?"

How much would that cost? Her thoughts were so scattered she couldn't remember how much her insurance deductible was. She might have to drive around with a damaged door for a while. But she needed to know what she was dealing with. "If he could give me an estimate, I'd appreciate it."

He went to get his cell phone out of his car, leaving her alone with Caleb.

He shoved his hands in his pockets, his gaze straying after Mason. "Something occurred to me, a possible reason for these weird break-ins where nothing is missing." He glanced down at her. "But you aren't going to like it."

Nothing could upset her more than she already was. Still, she braced herself. "Go on."

"It's obvious these guys are looking for something. And since they broke into your car after we parked it here last night, that means they didn't find it in your apartment."

"I don't have anything!" Her voice came out louder than she intended, fueled by frustration.

"Yes, you do." His soft tone sounded in sharp contrast to her outburst. "You have the notes that Fairmont wrote to your mother."

The import of his words struck at her like a fist. What if Mr. Fairmont really was her father? And what if he wanted to make sure those letters weren't seen by anyone—like his wife?

TEN

Darcie sat at Lauren's kitchen table and stared at the number displayed on her cell phone. As much as she dreaded doing it, she had to call Mr. Fairmont. Caleb and the others were right. This was the only step they could take toward freeing her from this nightmare.

Lauren sat beside her, and Caleb had taken Brent's chair at the end. Percy sat on the floor at his side, staring intently up at him.

Caleb stared at the little dog with a bemused expression. "What does it want from me?"

Darcie answered distractedly, "Attention. He likes you."

His look became perplexed. "Why?"

"Oh, come on." Lauren laughed at his obvious bewilderment. "You're a likable guy. I'll bet little kids like you, too."

"That's different," he said. "I like them back."

They both fell silent, and Darcie felt the weight of their stares. She had to do it. Delaying wouldn't accomplish anything.

Her finger pressed the call button.

"Fairmont Industries," said a pleasant female voice. "How can I direct your call?"

"I'd like to speak with Mr. Fairmont, please." She took comfort from the fact that her voice didn't tremble.

"Mr. Fairmont isn't in the office. May I ask what this concerns?"

Darcie bit her lip. "It's a personal matter."

Only a brief pause and then, "He isn't due back in the office until Friday, and his administrative assistant is off today as well. Would you like me to leave a message?"

She almost told the woman she'd call back another time, but the idea of gathering her courage a second time wasn't appealing.

"What about Mr. Mitchell? Is he in?"

"I believe so. One moment, please."

Caleb's eyebrows rose in a question.

She covered the phone with her free hand. "At least he knows who I am. Maybe he'll tell me when Mr. Fairmont will return."

The call was answered on the second ring. "Aaron Mitchell."

Darcie straightened in her chair. "Mr. Mitchell, this is Darcie Wiley." Silence. Didn't he remember her? "We met yesterday at Fairmont Estate. I'm the one who—"

"Yes, Ms. Wiley, I know who you are." Curiosity sounded clearly in his tone. "How can I help you?"

She swallowed against a dry throat. "I need to talk to Mr. Fairmont. I know he's out of town, and I wondered if you knew how to get in touch with him."

An even longer pause. "I have his cell phone number, but if you'll forgive me for saying this, I'm not sure he would appreciate me giving it out."

The statement hung between them like an unresolved minor chord on a keyboard. Darcie knew what he didn't say. Mr. Fairmont wouldn't appreciate Mitchell giving the number to *her*. She sagged against the chair and shot a defeated look toward Caleb. "I understand. When you talk to him next will you give him my number and ask him to call me?"

She must have sounded as down as she felt, for he answered in a kinder voice, "I can do that." He cleared his throat. "Actually, maybe I can do better than that. Can I call you back in a few minutes?"

"Yes, sure."

The line went dead. She set the phone on the table in front of her and stared at it.

"What'd he say?" asked Lauren.

"He's going to call back."

She gave them a quick review of their conversation. The phone rang before she finished.

"That didn't take long," Caleb commented as she snatched it up.

"Hello?"

"Ms. Wiley, it's Aaron Mitchell again. I just spoke with Richard. This isn't public knowledge, but he's cut his trip short and is on his way to Dulles to catch a flight back home. His plane lands at seven, and he says he can meet you here at the office at eight o'clock."

"Tonight?" Darcie shot straight out of her seat, alarm zinging down her spine. She thought she'd have a few days to prepare.

"He is planning to spend the next few days at home. Things are in something of an uproar there, as you can imagine." A delicate pause. "He didn't think it was a good idea for you to meet there."

"No, of course not." The idea of facing both Fairmonts at once sent a shudder rippling through her body. "Okay, then. I'll be there tonight at eight. And Mr. Mitchell?"

"Yes?"

She took a breath. "Thank you. I appreciate your help."

"You're welcome. Goodbye, Ms. Wiley."

When she hung up, Lauren stood and pulled her trembling body into a hug. "Are you okay? You're white as a sheet."

"I—I just didn't think it would happen this soon."

"It's better to get it over with." With a final squeeze, she released her. "This way you won't have that hanging over your head for days."

"And you won't be alone," Caleb reminded her. "I'm going with you."

"I know." She couldn't manage even a shaky smile. "That's the only reason I agreed to this to begin with."

* * *

The offices of Fairmont Industries, one of the largest carpet manufacturers in Georgia, were housed in a four-story building in Midtown. Only a few cars were scattered around the parking lot. As Caleb pulled into the visitor space nearest the entrance, Darcie stared at the building. The design was modern, all glass and steel. Though the sun had not yet set, it had sunk below the building across the street. Fairmont Industries stood in shadow. The windows were darkly tinted so no light shone in any of them. If anyone was inside they could probably see out, but no one outside could see in. With a start, she realized she'd thought the same thing yesterday afternoon standing beside the pool house at Fairmont Estate, right before she had met Caleb and found Jason Lewis's body. A sense of foreboding slid over her.

Caleb shut off the engine and removed the keys from the ignition. "You ready?"

No, she wanted to say.

Instead she said, "I don't know what to say to him. I can't walk into his office and blurt out, 'Are you my father, and are you trying to kill me?'"

"That probably wouldn't go over very well." His laugh was no doubt meant to lighten her mood, but it didn't work. He sobered. "Okay, what about this? You start out by assuring him you had nothing to do with Lewis's death. Then tell him what happened last night. Then mention the letters."

Darcie committed his instructions to memory. "Okay. I can do that." Her voice shook with nerves.

He spoke softly. "Don't worry. If you get tongue-tied, I'll help you out. But if you can be the primary talker, that'll be best. And one more thing. Take this." He pulled something out of his breast pocket and handed it to her.

Darcie inspected the small canister in her hand. It was pink, a little smaller than a travel-size hairspray. The right size to fit in her hand. On one end was a button atop a nozzle. An empty key ring dangled off the side.

"What is it, pepper spray?"

"That's right. Lauren carries it with her. She gave it to me for you before we left the house."

"Why do I need it?" Rather than comforting her, the small can increased her fear. "You'll be with me, right?"

"Of course." A reassuring smile appeared on his face, but when Darcie started to relax, it faded. "But we can't predict what's going to happen in there. So I want you to put this in your purse and keep it close. All right?"

Shaken, she nodded. Her purse had a place on the side for her cell phone, which she moved to an inside pocket. There. Now all she had to do was reach into that pocket, pull out the can and spray.

So why didn't she feel better?

The building's front lobby was as sterile as the exterior. Inside the door to the right was a sitting area with square, brown furniture arranged on a rectangle of thick carpet. The rest of the floor was covered in white tile. The *clack-clack* from Darcie's sandals echoed as if they were in a cavern as she and Caleb approached a plain blond wood reception desk.

The uniformed security guard greeted them, "May I help you?"

"We're here for a meeting with Mr. Fairmont." She clutched the shoulder strap of her purse. "He's expecting us."

The man nodded. "He told me you were coming. His office is on the fourth floor. When you exit the elevator, turn right and follow that hallway all the way to the end."

He waved them toward a set of elevators behind them, and, with a nod of thanks, they made their way to them.

Neither spoke during the short ride to the top floor. Darcie was preoccupied trying to plan what she would say to this man who might be her father, and Caleb seemed absorbed in tracking the progress of their ascent by way of the lights on the instrument panel.

When the doors slid open, she stepped onto a thickly carpeted floor. An eerie silence enveloped them. There wasn't a single sound from anywhere, not even the soft blowing of the air conditioner, though obviously the unit was working overtime. The chill of an artificial winter hung in the air.

Caleb folded his arms tightly across his chest. "Man, it's cold up here."

Though he spoke in a normal tone, the empty room absorbed and dulled his voice. Darcie looked over a field of chest-high cubicle walls, each one a sound barrier. Not a hint of movement anywhere.

She pointed to the right. "I guess we go that way."

As they walked she found herself tiptoeing so as not to break the silence. Which was ridiculous, since the thick carpet made noise from her sandals impossible. But the very stillness of the room increased her desire to stay as quiet and unnoticeable as she could.

At the end of the hallway, they encountered a row of real offices, the kind with walls and doors. A secretary's desk sat in front of each one. She might have wondered which way to turn, but she saw that the door to the corner office on her right stood open and a warm light shone from inside. That office was three times the size of the others.

"This must be the place." Her voice came out barely above a whisper.

In response, Caleb placed a large hand on her shoulder and gave her a comforting squeeze. Somehow, the gesture gave her the courage she needed to propel her feet forward. She paused outside of the open doorway, drew in a breath for courage and stepped inside.

Her first thought was that Mr. Fairmont had hired a different decorator for his office than his house. Though no less opulent, this room displayed more warmth and personality than any she'd seen in the mansion. Honey oak furniture gleamed in the warm light. Four tufted black leather chairs surrounded a small round table in one corner, and matching guest chairs faced the huge desk. Bookshelves lined one wall, and on the others hung photographs in a variety of oak frames. She glimpsed pictures of a man holding up a string of fish in one, a skier on a snow-covered mountain in another and a couple on horseback. She had a quick impression that the woman was a younger version of Mrs. Fairmont, but she didn't take the time to examine any of them. Her attention was fixed on the man seated behind the desk, bent over a stack of papers.

Richard Fairmont was an attractive man with an athletic build and thick silver hair. His face bore few signs of age, giving the impression that he had gone gray well before his time. The conservative white shirt he wore open at the collar had a freshly starched look, though she knew he had just gotten off an airplane. Had he gone to the trouble to change clothes for this meeting with her? Faint pleasure tickled in her stomach at the idea.

He looked up and caught sight of her. For a moment, he sat frozen, the paper in his hands completely still as he searched her face. Then an emotion passed over his features, a nostalgic look of familiarity. The paper fluttered back onto the stack, forgotten, and he rose slowly from his chair, his gaze holding hers.

"You could only be Darcie." His words carried a hint of wonder. "You look so much like your mother."

There was no doubt he meant it as a compliment. A cold place in Darcie's core warmed at his tone.

He became aware of Caleb, and she watched the slight smile fade as he inspected the big man at her side. His eyes narrowed almost imperceptibly for scarcely a second. The chair rolled away behind him as he rounded the corner of his desk toward them, hand outstretched.

"Hello. I'm Richard Fairmont." He shook Caleb's hand.

"Caleb Buchanan. I'm a friend of Darcie's. Nice to meet you, sir."

Mr. Fairmont turned to her, and the smile returned to linger around his lips. "Darcie. We meet at last." He sobered, and his expression became sorrowful. "Please accept my condolences on the passing of your mother. She was a fine woman and a wonderful mother, I'm sure."

"Thank you, sir. Yes, she was the best mom a girl could have."

Tears threatened, but with iron resolve Darcie refused to give in to them. Getting emotional would accomplish nothing and would only make her look like a weakling.

"Please take a seat." He gestured toward the table.

Darcie rolled one of the chairs back and slid into it. She felt like a child when she settled into the soft leather. The men selected places on either side of her.

When they were all seated, Mr. Fairmont folded his hands together and laid them on the table in front of him.

"When Aaron told me this afternoon that you'd requested to meet with me, I was pleased. I'd already decided to get in touch with you when I returned from DC." A pained expression overtook his face. "I'm so sorry you've become entangled in this mess with Lewis. Finding his body must have been traumatic for you."

She didn't hide her shudder. "One reason I wanted to talk with you was to assure you that I didn't have anything to do with Mr. Lewis's death."

In some tiny corner of her mind she'd hoped that word of the detective's suspicions had not reached him. In this she was disappointed. Instead of surprise, his look of sorrow deepened as he shook his head.

"Of course you didn't. I've told—" He caught himself. "I've told everyone that you are completely innocent, and I refuse to listen to any accusations against you."

No need to guess who he'd stopped himself from mentioning. No doubt Darcie had been the topic of at least one discussion with his wife.

"Thank you for that."

The sorrow evaporated, replaced by a smile that twisted his lips sideways. "Of course, my dear. I feel somewhat responsible, since it was my idea for you to work at the house. Obviously…"

He continued talking, but for a moment Darcie didn't hear his words. Sound stopped registering on her brain when she saw that smile. It was so familiar. She'd seen it a million times in the mirror. And now that she looked more closely at his eyes, their shape was astoundingly similar to hers as well.

He really is my father.

The pounding in her rib cage picked up volume, and she had to force herself to tune it out, to listen to his words.

"…here at the office. I'm not sure what, but I'm sure the human resources department can find something that will fit with your schedule when you return to school. And then when you've gotten your degree, we'll figure out a better placement. Does that sound good?"

She gave herself a little shake. "That's very kind of you."

What came next? She searched her thoughts for Caleb's instructions. *Assure him that you didn't kill Jason Lewis.* Check. She'd done that. She rubbed her sweaty palms on her capris beneath the table and cast a panicked glance sideways at Caleb.

With a slight nod that he understood, he spoke up. "Another reason Darcie requested this meeting was to tell you about some alarming things that happened to her last night."

That's it.

Mr. Fairmont's brows arched high. "Oh?" He looked at her for an explanation.

"My house and car were broken into, and then I was attacked in a restaurant parking lot."

Shock dawned on his features. "Are you all right? Were you harmed?"

"Just a few bumps and bruises. The police insist that the attack was random, but…" She caught her lip between her lips. "I know it sounds paranoid, but I think I've got something that someone wants."

He went very still, and then leaned toward her, holding her eyes with his. "What do you have?"

In the moment before she answered, his manner became tense, expectant.

She glanced at Caleb and found him watching her. The time had arrived to discuss the real reason they'd come. His slight nod urged her to continue.

Turning back to Mr. Fairmont, she forced herself to answer in a normal voice. "I'm not sure, but I think it may have something to do with some letters I found in my mother's things after she died." She paused. "Letters from you."

For a moment his face was completely blank. She watched his features change as realization dawned on him and the friendly, open expression became closed, distant.

He leaned back slowly in his chair. "You don't know, do you?"

"Know what?" She swallowed. "About my…my father?"

"That's why you're here. You want me to explain those letters."

Her hands trembled, and she clasped them together beneath the table. "Yes. I want to know what your relationship was with my mother." She gulped. "And with me."

No one spoke. Darcie watched the struggle of unnamed emotions on his face. The silence grew awkward, and beside her Caleb shifted in his seat.

She saw the moment when he came to a decision. The struggle stopped, and his expression became resigned, almost sad. His gaze rose from the tabletop to fix on Caleb's face. "If you don't mind, Mr. Buchanan, I'll ask you to step outside so I can talk to my—" His lips snapped shut for the space of a breath, and Darcie's pulse quickened. "To Darcie alone."

Caleb also leaned back in the chair and folded his arms across his chest, giving the impression of an immovable mountain. "No, sir."

Mr. Fairmont's voice became politely cold. "I beg your pardon?"

"I said no." His jaw hardened. "I'm not leaving her alone with you."

Anger flickered in Mr. Fairmont's eyes. "Surely you aren't accusing me of intending to harm her." When Caleb made no move, he sucked in a long breath and then let it out. "I am about to tell her something that has been a shameful secret in my family for twenty-two years, something less than a handful of people know. I don't know you. At this moment, I don't wish to know you. And I certainly am not going to air the Fairmont dirty laundry in your presence."

Dirty laundry? Was that how he thought of her? Darcie could have been angry, but instead she felt despair pressing on her. Her own father thought of her as a dirty secret to be kept. Her throat tightened around a painful lump. But at least he would do her the courtesy of sharing the secret.

And she desperately wanted to know.

Her purse sat in the chair beside her, the strap still hanging from her shoulder. She slung it off and pulled the purse into her lap. Beneath the table she slipped out the canister of pepper spray and held it in her hand.

Swiveling the chair slightly toward Caleb so he could see, she said, "I'll be all right."

She watched his eyes move as he studied the room. The only door was the one through which they'd entered. The floor-to-ceiling windows that lined one wall did not open.

Finally, he uncrossed his arms and stood. "I'll be right outside the door. If you need me, holler." He leveled a warning glare on Mr. Fairmont before he left, pulling the door closed behind him.

Darcie stared at the door, her bravado of a moment before melting away. She wasn't afraid of being physically hurt in this office. But the possibility of Mr. Fairmont inflicting a different kind of pain terrified her. Sometimes emotional wounds hurt a whole lot more.

ELEVEN

The click of the door closing had not died away before Mr. Fairmont shook his head. "That's quite a friend you've got there."

Now that she was alone with Mr. Fairmont, she felt more on edge and less inclined to friendly talk. "About those letters?"

"Ah, yes." A laugh floated out on a blast of breath. "I never dreamed Beth would keep them."

The can of mace grew warm in her hand. She leaned forward. "Mr. Fairmont, are you my father?"

"Me?" The surprise on his face was impossible to fake. "Is that what you think?"

Her voice shook when she answered. "I don't know what to think. All my life my mother told me my father had died in a car accident. But then I found the box with the letters." She lifted her free hand to press against her temple, where a pounding ache threatened.

To her surprise, he leaned forward and laid a hand gently on her arm. "She was telling the truth. I'm not your father, Darcie. I'm your uncle."

"My uncle?" Her body grew numb as her brain digested his words.

"That's right. Your father was my younger brother." He removed his hand and settled back into his chair. "Ryan was always a little wild. Today they'd probably diagnose him with some disorder or other, but in those days his teachers told my mother he was undisciplined and a troublemaker. Our father inherited a failing carpet manufacturing business from my grandfather when I was a boy, and he spent all his time working to build it into something strong. We didn't see much of him. Mother always had a soft spot for Ryan." He shrugged. "He was her baby, I guess. She didn't discipline him, or maybe she couldn't. He was quite a charmer." His eyes focused on a faraway thought. "Growing up I envied him. He was daring in a way I wasn't. He did exactly what he wanted, when he wanted."

What an odd feeling, to hear a description of the father she had never met. Darcie hung on every word.

"What did he look like?"

Mr. Fairmont smiled. "Me. We both took after Father."

That explained why her eyes and mouth were shaped like the man sitting beside her.

"Wait. I have a picture of him as a boy." He went to the wall behind his desk and took down a small framed photograph.

Darcie took it from him. A family portrait, with

the mother seated and her family gathered around her. Mr. Fairmont's father stood behind, one hand resting on his wife's shoulder. The older boy stood next to him, and in front of Richard was Ryan. As Darcie studied the face, a tenderness she hadn't expected warmed her heart. Her father. He'd been a handsome boy, thin with dark hair like his father and brother. But Ryan had a mischievous grin that made her own lips twitch in response. A charmer, Mr. Fairmont had said. Yes, she could see that.

"He was a handsome boy." Reluctantly, she handed the photo back to him. "I can see why Mama would be attracted to him."

His hand froze in the act of grasping the frame. Lines creased his forehead. "What makes you think she was attracted to him?"

Confused, Darcie shook her head. "I assumed. I mean, here I am."

Sympathy gathered in the dark eyes fixed on her. "Your mother wasn't in love with Ryan, Darcie." He spoke in a gentle voice. "She only met him an hour or so before you were conceived."

That made no sense. Mama was a lady and had the strongest morals of anyone Darcie had ever known. "I don't understand."

"Your mother was an employee of Fairmont Industries, a factory worker. By then Father had stepped into an advisory role and I had taken over running the company. Ryan was unreliable and something of a loose cannon, but he was family. I kept him on in the role Father had given him, directing the national sales team."

He raked his fingers through the thick hair on one side of his head. "Shortly after I assumed control of the company, I decided to throw a picnic to boost morale. We held it at the estate, and everyone in the company was invited. Ryan showed up late, as usual, and he was drunk. Might have been high on something as well, I don't know."

Her father was a drug user? This was unreal. With a growing sense of desperation Darcie saw the direction in which the story was going, and she wanted to clamp her hands over her ears. But she couldn't turn away now. She had to know the truth.

"Go on."

"Beth was a very attractive young woman, and apparently Ryan was taken with her. He offered to show her the house. I supposed she didn't want to be rude to the company president's brother, so she went with him." His expression became grim. "My mother found her thirty minutes later huddled on the floor in one of the guest bedrooms, crying. Her clothing had been torn, and she'd been raped."

Horror crept over her. Mama, raped by Ryan Fairmont.

I'm the result of rape?

Nausea churned deep in her belly. Frantically she clapped a hand over her mouth, willing her stomach to settle.

"Mother wanted to cover it up. She sent someone

for me and insisted that I handle the situation quietly without involving the police. Anything to protect her baby boy." He shook his head, disgusted. "Ryan was unrepentant and offered to write Beth a check to compensate her." A grudging respect showed in his grim smile. "She refused to be bought off. She allowed us to pay for her medical bills only. Not a cent more. She quit her job and moved to Indiana to get away from the Fairmonts."

"Then she discovered she was pregnant." Darcie couldn't manage anything more than a whisper. "With me."

Mr. Fairmont nodded. "She contacted Ryan, and he again offered to write her a check, this time for an abortion."

She knew her mother well enough to imagine her reply to that suggestion. "Mama didn't believe in abortion."

"I know. Ryan told me she was pregnant and he'd washed his hands of her. And then he was killed in an automobile accident."

"Was he drunk?" she asked.

"No. High as a kite on crack. He was only thirty years old. A wasted life." The sigh he heaved held a world of sorrow. Then he looked up at her again. "After the funeral I contacted your mother. I insisted that she let me help her. After all, you were a Fairmont." His smile became brittle. "She finally agreed to let me help ensure you were raised in a home where you wouldn't have to go without. The life of a single mother, a factory worker, isn't easy. But she insisted that you were *not* a Fairmont, that the Fairmonts were to have no part in your life. Ryan had told no one else about the pregnancy, and she swore me to secrecy. I wasn't to tell anyone, especially not my wife or my mother. Except for one or two close business associates who helped me keep the secret over the years, I've kept that promise."

Darcie closed her eyes and focused on taking slow, even breaths. *I will not throw up. I will not throw up.* The mantra helped to settle the nausea that roiled in her stomach.

She opened her eyes to find Mr. Fairmont watching her. "I'm very sorry. I know how upsetting this must be."

Upsetting? Surely the biggest understatement of the century. With an effort, she stuffed her emotions in the back of her mind. Time enough to deal with them later. Right now she needed answers.

"So obviously those notes were sent with payments of some kind."

He nodded. "I helped as much as Beth would let me."

"Do you have any idea who might want them badly enough to attack?"

"No." His eyes reflected complete certainty. "Only four people alive know of their existence. Two of us are in this room, and one is in prison." His lips twisted. "Your uncle is hardly in a position to act.

I'd trust the other one with my own life. There must be something else you have that those people want."

Her lungs deflated. This meeting wasn't unfolding like she had thought.

"I don't have anything. Well, except this." She held up her right hand to show him Mama's ring. "It was in the box with the letters. I…I assumed my father gave it to her."

With a sad smile, he shook his head. "I gave it to her. I told her it might go easier on her if people thought she was a widow. She refused to wear it, but I wouldn't take it back. I told her if she didn't want it, she could sell it."

Darcie looked at the tiny sparkling stones. "Surely it's not worth anything."

"Those are real emerald chips, though so small they aren't worth much. A couple of hundred dollars at the most." A smile spread across his lips. "It makes me happy to see you wear it."

Though no doubt he meant the comment to be endearing, she couldn't shake an uneasy feeling that settled over her. She'd thought the ring was a gift from her father, and now she was thankful that wasn't the case. Otherwise she would have torn it from her finger and flung it away. But the sentimentality she'd assumed accompanied the gift was somehow diminished, knowing it was given to help Mama perpetuate a lie.

Oh, Mama. What you must have gone through all those years.

* * *

Caleb stood beside the office door for a long time, his ear tuned toward the inside. He heard only the drone of voices, Darcie's high and feminine, Fairmont's low and rumbling. But he couldn't make out a single word.

At least they both sound calm. If I hear a shout, I'll be in there in an instant.

He paced a few feet away and then back again, just to give his legs something to do. Examined the photographs on the secretary's neat desk. Picked up a magazine from the table beside a guest chair.

A noise reached him. It sounded like a desk drawer being slid closed. His head snapped up while he listened intently. Not a loud sound and not from the direction of Fairmont's office. From somewhere else in this vast space of what he'd thought were deserted cubicles.

An eerie feeling crept up his spine. Obviously one wasn't as empty as he'd assumed.

Mr. Fairmont leaned back in his chair, his fingers intertwined and resting on his lean stomach. "I've wondered about the pup I sent your mother. Did he brighten her last days?"

Finally, a happier subject to discuss. Smiling, Darcie nodded. "Percy is a pure delight. Mama loved to watch his antics. He made us both smile."

"Good, good. You still have him?"

"Of course." She lowered her voice. "We've been through a lot together, Percy and me."

"And what about that collar that came with him. You have that as well?"

Something in his voice pricked her attention. A casual question, so then why did she detect a slight change in his tone?

"Yes, I still have it. He's never worn it, though."

"Of course not." He flicked a hand in the air. "Those collars were my wife's idea. Ridiculous, if you ask me. They're gaudy and flashy and far too big for the little dogs she breeds. She insists they're a status symbol, that they give her dogs prestige." He shook his head in an indulgently amused gesture. "So be sure to keep the ugly thing around, especially if you ever intend to sell the dog."

"Oh, I could never sell Percy." The idea was ludicrous. Percy was a member of her family.

The thought of family brought a flush of guilt, and Mrs. Fairmont's derisive words from yesterday returned. *"Why he felt any desire to hire a thief's niece, I can't imagine."*

As though he read her thoughts, Mr. Fairmont changed the subject with a question. "I've also wondered about your uncle. Is he doing well?"

A chill descended in the room at the mention of Uncle Kenneth. "I have no idea. I've had no contact with him at all, except the note I sent telling him when Mama passed." She forced herself to look up from the table and into his eyes. "I hope you and your wife don't hold my uncle's crimes against me. I would never, ever steal. My mother raised me to know right from wrong."

His gaze softened. "Of course you wouldn't. The thought never entered my mind. As for Olivia." His tone turned cold. "Don't worry about what she thinks. Her opinion doesn't sway mine at all, in this or any other matter."

How sad for a husband and wife to be so distant. Though Darcie had no positive role model for healthy marriage in her own family, she'd envied her friends who had parents who'd loved each other.

"Thank you," she said.

"I mentioned that there are only four people who know the secret of your parentage. Obviously Kenneth is one of them." He speared her with a direct gaze. "Did your mother have much contact with Kenneth after he went to prison?"

A simple question. Why, then, did his voice become so tense when he asked it?

"She wrote him regularly, but as far as I know he never wrote back."

"And you would have found the letters if he had, wouldn't you?" The tight voice stirred a sense of unease in Darcie. She noticed that his hands were clasped so hard his knuckles showed white beneath his tanned skin.

"If she'd kept them I would have," she replied.

"He's due to be released in a few months, isn't he?" The intensity in his gaze made her squirm.

"I'm not really sure, to be honest. I've purposefully avoided knowing anything about Uncle Kenneth."

"You'll forgive me if I offer a piece of advice?" She nodded, and he leaned forward. "If there's a wasp in the room with you, it's a good idea to pay attention to where he is."

From his grim expression, he'd learned that lesson the hard way. Of course he had. From Uncle Kenneth, the man who had betrayed him.

"When he is released, he may contact you." He held her gaze in a firm stare. "When he does, let me know. All right?"

Darcie wasn't sure whether she was more disturbed by the urgency in his voice or the idea that Uncle Kenneth may contact her. She squirmed in her chair and gave a shaky nod.

His hands relaxed. Smiling, he rested them on the arms of his chair. "Good. Because now that you know the secret of your parentage, I'd like to acknowledge you publicly as family."

The idea was so alarming Darcie shrank against the opposite side of her chair. "Are…are you sure that's a good idea?"

"Why wouldn't it be?" Understanding dawned on his features. "We wouldn't have to expose the details of your conception. Only the fact that you are my niece." His smile became paternalistic. "Olivia and I have no children. It would make me happy to have a relationship with you. You could call me Uncle Richard. Think about it?"

More disturbed than at any point during this extremely disturbing conversation, Darcie nodded. An overwhelming desire to flee took possession of her. She had to get out of here, to be alone and think about all she'd learned.

Beneath the cover of the table, she slid the pepper spray back into the pocket of her purse and then made a show of slipping the strap over her shoulder.

"I need to go. It's getting late, and you've just gotten back into town."

He rose when she did, and for one horrified moment she thought he might embrace her. She hurried toward the door. When her hand touched the knob, his soft voice stopped her.

"Darcie."

She looked up to find that he had not moved, but stood beside the table with a tender smile fixed on her.

"Thank you for coming. I'm glad everything is out in the open between us."

A painful knot had lodged in her throat, clogging her words. She managed a nod before she twisted the doorknob and left.

The office door opened, and Caleb looked up from the magazine he'd been leafing through. Darcie emerged alone, her eyes troubled and heavy creases in the soft skin between her brows. Her hands hugged the strap of her purse against her body like a shield.

"Everything okay?" he asked.

She flashed him a quick smile along with a shaky nod. "Let's just get out of here."

Caleb glanced at the open office doorway. Fairmont hadn't physically hurt her, but whatever he'd said had upset her a lot. With a protective hand on her back, he guided her down the hallway.

The creepy silence had returned to the office building. No more drawers sliding shut. Still, as they walked toward the elevators, he imagined the menacing weight of a stare on the back of his neck. He glimpsed over his shoulder expecting to see Fairmont standing in his office door, glaring after them. But the doorway was empty.

TWELVE

The first part of the drive back to the Emersons' home was silent. Though Caleb itched to ask about the family secret that had forced him out of the room, he would not press her to talk about it. That learning it had upset Darcie was obvious. Sooner or later the team would need to know…but there was no reason to make her go through everything twice. He glanced at her. She sat sideways in her seat, staring out the window. Headlights of passing cars reflected off her silky hair, and once he saw her shoulders heave. Every now and then he heard a soft sob, and the urge to pull over and gather her into a comforting hug was almost overpowering. And that made him angry.

My task in this job is to keep her safe. Period. That's what I promised. Nothing more.

But surely his Christian duty was to comfort those who mourn. Given the chance, he'd offer comfort to a stranger who was in obvious distress. Why not someone he knew and cared about?

The thought slapped at him, and his head jerked backward against the headrest.

She's someone I know. *Not someone I care about.*

Only a cold, hard-hearted person could not feel sympathy toward someone who had gone through the things Darcie had in the past two days.

Well, okay, maybe I care. I care about a lot of people.

The admission stirred a worry to the surface of his mind. No matter how he justified it, caring for Darcie was different than caring about a stranger on the street. The danger lay in that difference. He cast a hurt glance upward through the windshield, toward the blackness of heaven.

The only reason I agreed to help her is because of You, Lord. I told You I didn't want to, and You made me. Are You putting me out there to get hurt again?

Somewhere in the recesses of his spirit, Caleb knew God loved him. But surely a God who cared wouldn't send him into a situation where he was so vulnerable. Where he could have his heart broken again.

No, the God he knew wouldn't do that. So that meant maybe God didn't push him into this job after all. Maybe he'd done it himself. The idea was alarming on so many levels.

But I heard You. I felt You nudge me to befriend her, to help her. Didn't I?

No answer but another soft sob from Darcie's side of the pickup. Above him stretched a sky of unbroken blackness, a void into which he threw his prayer only to have it disappear.

Maybe he hadn't heard God after all. Maybe he'd mistaken his own inner voice for God's. And now he'd gotten himself into a mess, one that might end up with his heart broken so badly it would never mend.

Caleb's thoughts were interrupted by a sniffle, and Darcie twisted around in her seat.

"He's not my father." Though the cab was dark, the dashboard lights glittered off of her wet cheeks. "I wish he were. He's my uncle."

Her uncle. "So your mother was his sister?"

Locks of hair waved around her face when she shook her head. "No, my father was his brother. He—" a sob broke her voice "—raped my mother."

Caleb's hands clenched into fists around the steering wheel. Of all the slimy scum in the world, men who hurt women were at the bottom of the heap.

Darcie's soft cries touched something deep in him, and he removed one hand from the steering wheel to cover hers. "I'm sorry."

"My father was a drug user and a rapist. When I think of what my mother endured…" Tears choked off her voice.

Caleb squeezed. "Don't. It won't help her, and it will only torture you."

Gulping staccato breaths of air, she nodded and made a visible effort to get control of herself. "I can't help but wonder. Was I a constant reminder of the brutality she suffered? When she looked at me, did she see the man who attacked her?"

"Stop that." Caleb gave her hand a shake. "Of course not. Your mother loved you, you know that. You told Fairmont that she was the best mom a girl could have. If she thought of you only as a result of that attack, she couldn't have loved you deeply enough to be that great mom, could she?"

A flicker of hope showed in the eyes she raised to his. "No." A sniff. "No, she couldn't. She did love me."

"Of course she did. I'll venture to say you were the person she loved most in her life. Don't you think?"

A trembling smile appeared in the midst of the shadows that hid most of her face. "She used to tell me I was the best blessing God ever gave her." A shuddering breath. "How could that be true, when she had to go through such a horrible experience to have me?"

"I know the answer to that." He glanced away from the road at her. "Mind if I quote a little Scripture?"

"Okay." She sounded cautious.

"*We know that all things work together for good to them that love God, to them who are called according to His purpose.* Paul wrote that to the church in Rome."

He could almost hear her mind turning the Scripture over in the short silence that followed.

Finally she shook her head. "I don't get it. Mama loved God, but she wasn't called to any purpose. She wasn't a preacher or a missionary or anything."

Caleb smiled. She might have been him a few years ago, questioning God's plan for his life. "God has a plan for everyone. Even when bad things happen, He'll turn it into something good for us. Maybe part of His plan for your mom was to be your mother. Not that He wanted her to suffer, but when she did He turned that suffering into something good." He spoke softly. "I'll bet she thought of you as something good that God gave her."

The tremble in her lip disappeared, and a real smile broke free. "Thank you for that." She tilted her head to one side, studying him. "Your faith is really strong, isn't it?"

Caleb kept his eyes forward. Yesterday morning he would have agreed. But tonight doubts twisted his gut into knots, and his spirit was troubled by a single thought: if he couldn't even be sure of hearing God's voice over his own, apparently his faith wasn't as strong as he thought.

Darcie tossed fitfully in bed that night. A dozen times she replayed the meeting with Mr. Fairmont, or Uncle Richard as he wanted to be called. She re-examined every word and writhed on the mattress at the thought of her mother being hurt. In her mind's eye she saw Mama, young and beautiful, crouched on the floor in a spare bedroom at the Fairmont mansion, sobbing at the violence just done to her. Just yesterday morning she had sat in the kitchen of that same house polishing silver, unaware that she had come into being in the midst of a savage attack in one of the upstairs rooms. Her thrashing legs became entangled in the sheets. Percy, grumbling, moved to the far edge of the bed to get away from her.

Uncle Richard. His face loomed in the darkness of the bedroom. If her father had lived, he would have looked like Uncle Richard. Though certainly she wouldn't have glimpsed compassion in those dark eyes. She wouldn't have seen kindness, as she had in the eyes of her uncle.

Yet there had also been something disturbing, something she could not identify. When he spoke of Uncle Kenneth as a wasp to be watched, the tension in his face had been nearly palpable. And when he made her promise to let him know if Kenneth contacted her, she'd detected a sense of urgency that made her squirm again, hours later and miles away from the meeting. Was he simply a protective uncle worried that his newly acknowledged niece would be hurt by the same man who had betrayed him? Or was there something more?

And what was behind the request to make their relationship public?

Maybe he really does want to claim me because he never had a child of his own. He wants to know

*that the Fairmonts won't die out when he is gone,
but will live on in another generation.*

Her eyes flew open as another thought occurred
to her.

Maybe he wants an heir.

The idea snatched her breath. The Fairmonts were
among the wealthiest people in the state of Georgia. Who knew how much Fairmont Industries was
worth? He probably had other assets as well, investments and so on. Rich people did. And then there
was the family estate.

*Could I ever live in that house, knowing my
mother had been brutalized there?*

Nausea returned at the thought. No, she'd sell it,
or maybe turn it into a historical site.

What am I thinking?

A guilty flush erupted over her whole body when
she realized the turn her thoughts had taken. Her
mother had spent her whole life sheltering Darcie
from knowing the harsh reality behind her conception, and here she was calmly planning what she
would do if she inherited Fairmont Estate. Maybe
she was more like Uncle Kenneth than she thought.
The idea made her sick with shame.

The last time she looked at the clock on the nightstand, the display read 4:27 a.m.

*I ought to just go ahead and get up. Sleep isn't
going to happen tonight.*

That was the last thing she remembered before
she fell into an exhausted sleep.

* * *

Bang bang bang.

The sound reverberated from some other part of the house. Darcie sat straight up in bed, heart thudding in her chest. What was it? A break-in? Her pulse went from sleepy to panicky in the span of a few seconds. Had the people who'd attacked her and chased her and Caleb found her?

Outside, the sun had risen, and it spilled early morning light through the window into the comfortable bedroom. The clock read 6:54 a.m. On the mattress beside her, Percy leaped up and ran to the edge of the bed, yapping like crazy.

"Percy, shhh!" Straining her ears, she heard the sound of voices below. Brent's deep tone, then another male voice, then a third. She couldn't make out the words, but then she heard the unmistakable sound of the front door closing. Were those footsteps on the hardwood entry hall?

A soft rap on her door startled her. She jumped as the door opened and then blew out a breath when Lauren's face appeared.

But she only relaxed for a second, because her friend wore a grave expression. "Darcie, you need to get dressed. There's someone here to see you."

A list of possible visitors flashed through her brain. Caleb? No, Lauren wouldn't look so solemn. Uncle Richard, maybe?

"Who is it?" she asked as she slid out of bed and reached for her duffel bag and clean clothes.

Lauren replied in an unhappy tone. "It's the police. Something terrible has happened, and they want to talk to you."

"We seem to be seeing a lot of each other in the past few days, Ms. Wiley." Detective Samuels had seated himself in one of Lauren's comfortable living room chairs. Two patrolmen stood sentinel behind him, their expressions hard as cement.

Perched on the edge of a couch cushion facing the detective, Darcie eyed him with caution. Given the choice she wouldn't spend any more time with this man than she had to. In fact, she'd give a great deal to never see him again. Unfortunately, the choice was not hers to make.

"We certainly are." She kept her voice clear of emotion, acutely aware that every word she uttered would be weighed and examined.

He waited for a moment, watching her with an expectant air.

What are you doing here at seven o'clock in the morning? The question nearly burst from her lips, but she held it back. Judging by his relaxed but alert posture, Samuels intended to steer this conversation at his own pace. The wisest course was to let him.

After an uncomfortable moment, he leaned back and rested his arms along the cushioned arms of the chair. "I need to ask you a few questions about your activities last night."

She glanced sideways at the empty doorway. Were

Brent and Lauren hovering nearby, listening? If only they'd been allowed to stay, she might have drawn courage from their presence. But the detective had insisted on speaking with her alone, so they'd taken Percy and left the room. "I was here most of the evening."

Samuels leaped on the word like a cat on a bird. "Most?"

"I left here at seven-thirty for a meeting and got back a little after nine."

"A meeting with whom?"

Red flags waved in her mind's eye. Would it look suspicious to say she'd met with the man who owned the property on which she had found Lewis's body? Best to answer with prudence.

"It was a personal matter."

He stroked his chin with a finger. "Now I wonder about that. I wonder a lot. What personal business did you have with Richard Fairmont?"

The stiffness wilted from Darcie's shoulders. He knew she'd visited Uncle Richard. Was he having her followed?

"I—" She swallowed. *Choose the words carefully.* "I was—"

A sound interrupted from the direction of the entry hall. The front door opened. Heads turned toward the doorway to the living room as Caleb burst into sight, chest heaving as though he'd run there. The eyes he fixed on Darcie were filled with emotion.

"I'm sorry. I'm so sorry." Fingers splayed, he held

his hands toward her in a halting gesture. "Don't worry. We'll figure this out."

Bewildered, Darcie shook her head. "Sorry about what? Figure what out?"

Caleb's gaze jerked toward Detective Samuels. "You haven't told her?"

"I was about to."

Elbows planted on the arms of the chair, he intertwined his fingers and rested his hands in his lap. If he'd watched her closely a moment before, his gaze now could only be described as intense.

"Richard Fairmont was murdered in his office last night." His smile became brittle. "It seems, Ms. Wiley, that you were the last person to see him alive."

THIRTEEN

A shocked silence met Samuels's announcement. Caleb closed his eyes against the horror carved into Darcie's face.

Samuels had showed up at his house at six-thirty that morning, demanding to know where Darcie was. When he told Caleb the reason, what could he do? He'd had no choice but to tell the detective what he wanted to know. Though Caleb had gotten dressed in a hurry and covered the distance between his house and Brent's at breakneck speed, Samuels beat him.

If only I'd gotten here before them, I could have prepared her. Not that anything could ready her to hear of the death of the uncle she'd just discovered.

But the worst was yet to come.

Ignoring the detective, he crossed the room and lowered himself to the cushion beside her. The violent trembling of her body when he placed his arm across her shoulders stirred up such a fierce sense of protection that his jaws clenched tight.

"I don't understand." Her voice was high, tight, like a little girl struggling not to cry. "I just saw him. How could he be…dead? Who could have killed him?"

"That's what we're here to find out." Samuels rested one leg across the other, his hands looped around his knee.

"Here?" She drew a shuddering breath. "I don't know anything. How could I? He was fine when I left him."

"Was he?" His expression became almost fierce. "Can you prove that?"

The shivering stopped and her shoulders stiffened. "Surely you don't think I killed him? I would never—I couldn't—" Her head jerked toward Caleb. "You were there. Tell them."

Miserable, Caleb scrubbed a hand across his mouth. Why, oh why had he agreed to leave that office?

He squeezed her arm as he delivered the blow. "Darcie, I can't."

"What?" Alarm crept into her voice. "What do you mean?"

He spoke softly, gripping her shoulder as though that would somehow soften the blow. "I never saw Fairmont again after I left his office. The two of you were in there alone, and then you came out. He didn't."

Horror dawned on her face. With a lurch, she wrenched away from his hand and vaulted off the couch. The look of betrayal she turned on him shot straight through his ribs and found its mark deep in his heart.

A loud buzzing in Darcie's ears drowned out her thoughts. Her chest heaved with the attempt to catch an elusive breath. When the room began to spin, she doubled over, hands resting on her knees for support.

"Lauren!"

Caleb's shout echoed in the room, and a moment later Lauren's gentle arms were around her, guiding her back to the couch. When she sank onto the cushions, Lauren continued to hold her close.

"It's all right. It's going to be all right." Her friend's soft croon seeped past the buzzing. "Darcie, listen to me. You can handle this. Calm down. You didn't do anything wrong, and we will prove it."

She forced herself to listen to the calming voice, to draw a long, slow breath into her lungs. Then another.

Richard Fairmont dead. Just last night he had asked her to call him Uncle Richard, asked if he could claim her publicly as his niece.

It's not fair!

Her hands balled into fists, and she wanted to beat them against something. Her legs. The couch arm. Caleb. She looked up and spied him standing over her, watching with a helpless expression. Anger flared to life so vividly she had to struggle to stop from flying at him. He'd promised to help her, to keep her safe. *Liar!*

That's not fair. He's only telling the truth.

She wanted to ignore the whisper of reason, but she couldn't. The scene last night replayed in her mind. She'd said goodbye to Uncle Richard. What were his last words to her, the last ones she would ever hear him utter? *I'm glad things are out in the open between us.* The memory wrenched her heart. She'd left, while he had remained beside the little table. Waiting outside the office, Caleb could not possibly have seen him.

He could have lied for me, she thought sullenly.

But she knew the thought would never occur to the man his friends called Preacher Man. Dishonesty was not in his nature.

This wasn't Caleb's fault. He'd done what he could for her. One look at the misery in his face proved that.

Something relaxed inside her. A fist of anxiety still gripped her insides and no doubt would continue to do so until this whole nightmare was behind her. But at least she wasn't going through it alone. With a gentle pressure on Lauren's hands, she smiled both her gratitude and the message that she had regained at least a modicum of control. She couldn't quite manage a smile for Caleb, but she did give him a quick nod. He visibly relaxed.

When she looked at the detective, she caught a flicker of doubt in those steely eyes. Was he questioning his assumption that he had the killer in his sights? The flicker disappeared immediately, but the glimpse gave her the courage she needed to straighten her shoulders and face the man.

"I'm sorry." Her voice choked on the words, and she drew another fortifying breath. "It's the shock. I still can't believe he's gone." She looked directly into the man's eyes, willing him to see the truth. "I didn't kill him, Detective. When I left that office he was alive."

The man's eyes narrowed as he weighed her words. Though he didn't accept or dispute her claim, at least he didn't openly accuse her of lying. Not yet, anyway.

"Why were you there at all? What was this meeting about?"

"I wanted to assure him that I had nothing to do with Mr. Lewis's death."

"You could have done that on the telephone."

She bowed her head, acknowledging the comment. That was only a small part of the reason she'd requested the meeting. Her gaze flicked toward Caleb. Should she tell Detective Samuels about the notes? Then the whole ugly story would emerge, and she wasn't sure she wanted to make that public now. Maybe never.

Caleb watched her for a long moment and then faced the detective. "I advised Darcie to contact Mr. Fairmont."

"We all did." Lauren relaxed the tight hug, though

her hand remained comfortingly on Darcie's arm. "She had some questions that needed to be answered."

Samuels's jaw tightened. "What kind of questions?"

The truth would come out sooner or later. She might as well be as transparent as she could. Maybe the detective would believe her if he sensed that she was holding nothing back.

"I wanted to ask Mr. Fairmont if he was my father."

Throughout the story, Darcie held the detective's gaze steadily. She told him everything she'd told Caleb and his friends…well, almost everything. Though the words to describe the circumstances surrounding her mother's pregnancy were on the tip of her tongue, she bit them back. What purpose would it do to go into the sordid details? Let him think Mama had a brief affair with Ryan Fairmont before he died. Mama was beyond caring.

As she spoke, Samuels sat with his elbows planted on the chair's arms, his steepled fingers tapping rhythmically against one another. When she had described as much of her conversation with her uncle as she could remember, his fingers stilled.

"May I see the notes?"

Darcie nodded, and Lauren released her to stand. "I'll get them."

She left the room. In another part of the house came the faint sound of a door opening, and in the next minute Brent's harsh whisper was audible.

"Hey! You can't go in there. Come back here."

Percy charged into the room. Brent, bent over with outstretched hands, was hot on his heels. The little dog ran straight to Darcie and with one giant leap, landed in her lap. He planted his paws on her legs, faced the detective and proceeded to fill the air with ferocious yaps that left no doubt he intended to protect her with teeth and claws if necessary.

"Sorry," Brent mumbled, coming toward her to retrieve the captive. "He got away from me."

When Brent reached for him, Percy yelped and dove beneath Darcie's arm, hiding his face against her side. Darcie started to pick him up and hand him to Brent but then changed her mind. It was easy to muster the courage to answer the rest of the questions with Percy's reassuring presence in her lap.

"He'll be all right," she told Brent, who shrugged and retreated to stand along the wall behind the sofa.

Detective Samuels stared at the dog. "That dog looks a lot like the ones at Mrs. Fairmont's kennels."

"He's the same breed." Darcie buried her fingers in Percy's soft fur. "He was a gift from Uncle Richard to my mother last year, when she got so sick."

The man's gaze became speculative. "Does Mrs. Fairmont know you have one of her dogs?"

Discomfort nibbled at her. "I don't know." If she did, would she demand Percy back? Darcie's hand rested possessively on the dog's back.

Lauren returned with the shoe box. Darcie opened the lid and pulled the banded stack of notes out.

Those she handed to Detective Samuels; then she replaced the lid and set the box on the floor beside the sofa.

He flipped through them quickly. "These accompanied payments?"

She nodded. "Before you ask, I don't know how much or anything else about them. My mother didn't have a lot of money. I'm sure she used them to pay the bills." A thought dawned on her. Mama had paid her college tuition for the two years she attended without a second thought. When Darcie suggested getting a job to help with the bills, she had refused to consider it, insisting that Darcie needed to focus on her studies. When questioned, she said vaguely that Darcie's father had made arrangements for her education. "I think she might have used some of the money to pay for my college."

He shuffled the notes into a neat stack and replaced the rubber band, then handed them to one of the officers standing behind him. "I'll need to keep these." It was not a question.

Darcie bit back a protest. That stack of notes was one of the few things of her mother she had, and the only thing from Uncle Richard. Well, except…

She buried her right hand in Percy's fur to hide Mama's ring. She wouldn't give that up willingly.

Standing beside the couch, Caleb folded his arms across his chest. "What happens now? Are you finally going to listen to us about Darcie's apartment and car being searched and the kidnapping attempt?"

The detective's expression hardened. "What I do next is not your concern." He glanced around the room, including Brent and Lauren in the statement. "I told you Monday night to stay out of this investigation, but did you listen? No. And now a second man is dead." His glare settled on Caleb. "I ought to arrest you."

Caleb's face did not change, but his fingers bit into the flesh of his arms. "I'm not going to stand around with my fingers in my ears while someone shouts false accusations at one of my friends."

Though soft, his tone bore a fierce determination that made Darcie want to weep with relief. Caleb wasn't going to let her face this alone.

Samuels's face darkened and his lips pressed together. After a moment, he stood. "If you really want to help your friend, you might find her a good lawyer." He looked at Darcie, any hint that he believed her protestations of innocence absent from his manner. "I told you this before, and I'm telling you again. Don't leave town. I want to know where you are every minute."

Alarm nipped at her heels. "But I've told you, I didn't kill Uncle Richard. You've got to keep looking for the real killer."

"Oh, I'll get to the bottom of this eventually. Have no fear about that. In the meantime, you're still my number one suspect, Ms. Wiley."

She'd known that, of course, but to hear the words

from the lips of a police detective hit her with the weight of a load of wet concrete. "But…but why?"

At first she thought he wouldn't answer. His lips clamped together beneath eyes hardened by suspicion. Then he seemed to change his mind.

"Because I know the contents of Richard Fairmont's will." He leaned forward until his face was no more than a foot from hers and spoke in a low, calculated voice. "Your uncle left you half a million dollars, Ms. Wiley. Men have been killed for far less."

FOURTEEN

After delivering his verbal bomb, the detective swept out of the room. Caleb heard the front door close and tracked the man's progress through the front window. He slid into the passenger seat of one of the two police cruisers. The vehicles backed out of the driveway and sped away.

Darcie sat motionless on the sofa, staring at the floor in front of her feet. Jaw slack, lips parted, her eyes had the glaze of disbelief. He exchanged a glance with Brent, who lifted his shoulders in a shrug. The news had taken them all by surprise, though it made sense for Fairmont to provide for his niece in his will, since he had also provided for her during his life.

"Half a million dollars," Darcie repeated the figure in a distant voice. "Wow."

"It's a lot of money." Lauren dropped to the couch beside her. "He must have cared about you very much."

"I wish he'd told me years ago. I'd have liked to get to know him." She splayed the fingers of her right hand in front of her, and Caleb realized she was staring at her ring. "But Mama wouldn't let him. And now it's too late." Tears sparkled in her eyes.

Caleb seated himself in the chair Samuels had occupied, the one facing her. "Let's keep a cool head. We need to focus on getting you out of this."

"Do I need to hire a lawyer like he said?" She shook her head. "I don't know where to start."

Brent took the armchair next to Caleb. "We know a couple of good ones. I'll make some calls."

She turned a grateful look on him.

"In the meantime," Caleb said, "this cranks up the heat on our investigation."

Her head snapped toward him, disbelief clear on her features. "You mean you're going to keep investigating even after Detective Samuels told you not to?"

"Do you want us to stop?"

Her eyes went round. Silently, she shook her head.

Lauren relaxed, and Brent slapped his hands together, eagerness plain on his face. "Great. We move forward."

"Don't worry," Caleb told Darcie, "we'll stay out of Samuels's way. We don't want to interfere with the police. And if we find something relevant—"

"*When* we find something relevant," Lauren corrected.

Caleb acknowledged the comment with a nod. "We'll turn it over to him. What we need to do is figure out what rocks they won't look under. That's where we'll focus our efforts."

Tears once again glittered in Darcie's eyes, and she turned a quivering smile on all of them. "I can't thank you enough."

When she looked at him, Caleb held her gaze. "That's what friends are for."

Lauren and Brent both nodded. Darcie's smile softened, and Caleb's pulse did a weird quickstep in response.

Brent broke the moment. "All right then. What's our next step?"

"Let's start by figuring out what questions we need to have answered." Lauren held up a hand. "I mean besides the obvious, *who killed Richard Fairmont*?"

Caleb threw out the first one. "Did the same person who killed Fairmont also kill Lewis?"

Brent nodded. "Good one, but we can't answer it yet. What about this one—was the attack on Darcie the other night really to kidnap her or to force her to turn over those letters?"

"We can't answer that unless we get our hands on the attackers." Caleb flexed his fists. Those scumbags had better hope he didn't find them before Samuels did. "And how do we know for sure that the letters are what they're after?"

"We don't," said Lauren. "It's an assumption, but it's the only one we have."

Darcie's head turned toward each person as they spoke. "I have a question. How did Detective Samuels know the contents of Uncle Richard's will? He only died last night."

"Hmm." Caleb rubbed a finger across his lips, thinking. "His wife maybe?"

"That's possible," said Brent. "If she knew about the money but didn't know about Ryan, she might suspect the same thing we did, that her husband was Darcie's father."

Lauren nodded slowly. "That would explain her dislike."

"And she would definitely have told the police of her suspicions when Uncle Richard was killed." Crooked lines appeared on Darcie's smooth brow. "Should I call her? Tell her what I've discovered about my real father?"

Caleb weighed the question. "Normally I'd say yes, but I have a feeling Samuels would consider that a direct interference with his investigation."

A relieved sigh escaped from Darcie. No doubt that was an encounter she was happy to avoid as long as possible.

"That brings up another question." Brent heaved himself out of the chair and began to pace. "Who else knew about Darcie's relationship to Fairmont?"

Caleb saw where he was going. "Her other uncle, Kenneth."

"But he can't be involved," Darcie argued. "He's been in prison for almost five years. Now, if this had happened a few months from now—" A hand rose to cover her mouth, eyes wide.

"What?" Caleb leaned toward her and rested his elbows on his knees. "What have you remembered?"

"Something Uncle Richard said." Her eyes squinted, as though trying to focus on something not in the room. "He said Uncle Kenneth was scheduled to be released in a few months, and if he makes any attempt to contact me I should tell him." Her gaze focused on his face. "He asked me if Mama or I've had any contact with him while he was in prison. I told him no, but he seemed really tense when he brought up Uncle Kenneth."

"That's to be expected, don't you think?" Lauren asked. "I mean, the man stole hundreds of thousands of dollars from him."

Darcie shook her head. "There was more to it than that. He wanted to know if Mama had kept any letters from her brother, and there was this…" She grasped for a word and then shrugged. "I don't know, this kind of intense feeling about him for a few minutes. It wasn't there the rest of the time."

"Sounds to me like we just identified our next step. We need to talk to Pryor." Brent ceased his pacing. "Caleb, did you apply for that special visitor pass to Hancock State Prison yet?"

"I put in a call to a friend down there, but he hasn't called me back yet."

"Maybe you should call him again."

"No, I don't think so," Caleb said. "I've got some bigger strings to pull. Let me make another call."

* * *

Darcie handed her driver's license to Caleb, who passed it through the pickup's window. The prison guard studied it closely, then bent to look into the truck at her. Darcie forced herself to return his gaze calmly, though the pounding of her heart was so loud surely he could hear it and know how nervous she was. With another glance at the licenses, he handed them back through the window and waved them forward. The metal gate swung open, and Caleb pulled slowly through the tall fence that stretched around the desolate prison compound. As she passed, Darcie inspected the huge roll of barbed wire that topped the fence. Correction. That was not normal barbed wire. The barbs were longer, sharper and far more menacing. Razor wire. The term stepped forward from memory. Yes, that's what it looked like. A tangled mass of razors. She shuddered as they left the fence behind.

"How did you manage to get us in so quickly?" She glanced at Caleb's profile. "Didn't Mason say it might take weeks to get approved for a visit?"

"Normally it does." He flashed an appealing grin her way. "But I'm not normal."

She chuckled with him, and then he continued, "I met the warden a year or so ago, when his son got involved with the wrong crowd. He ended up in juvvie, where I hang out sometimes."

She eyed him skeptically. "You hang out at the Juvenile Detention Center?"

"Sometimes." The shoulder closest to her lifted in a shrug. "I go there and talk to the kids. Tell them what it's like to get crossways of the law and where they could end up if they don't get their acts together. Some of them listen to me when they won't listen to their parents or a judge or a cop."

That was understandable. She eyed the tattoos on his arms. She'd gotten so accustomed to them that she didn't even notice them anymore, but when she had first spied him kneeling by the water spigot on Fairmont Estate, they might as well have been flashing in neon. Between those tattoos and his massive size, she'd been a little frightened of him. That was before she'd come to know what a caring man he was, a gentle giant.

"I'll bet," was all she said.

"The warden's son's a good kid. He was just going through some stuff. You know, rebelling like all kids do. He took a liking to me, and I helped him get straightened out. He'll graduate from high school in a couple of weeks, and then he's going to Emory in the fall."

"Wow." Emory was one of the top-ranked schools in the state of Georgia. "No wonder the warden let us in on short notice. He owes you."

But Caleb shook his head. "He doesn't owe me a thing. But that business with his son introduced us, and now I count him among my friends. I'm not cashing in on a debt. I'm just asking a friend to help me out."

The matter-of-fact manner in which he spoke impressed Darcie more than the words. "You must have a lot of friends."

His grin returned. "You can never have too many."

They parked the pickup and walked through a series of gates. Darcie hung close to Caleb, whose confidence told her he was on familiar territory here. Did he visit other prisoners, young men in trouble who had not listened to his cautions, perhaps? She wouldn't be at all surprised.

Inside the building they stepped into a large waiting room, with chairs lining the walls. In the center a trio of guards sat behind a rounded desk. Caleb approached and gave his name to the one in the middle.

The man studied him with interest. "The warden told us you were coming. You're here to see Kenneth Pryor?"

"That's right. And this is Darcie Wiley, Pryor's niece."

The ease in Caleb's voice did nothing to settle Darcie's taut nerves as the guard inspected their driver's licenses. She dreaded talking to her uncle more than anyone else in the world, with the possible exception of Detective Samuels.

He set their ID cards on the desk in front of him and pulled a computer keyboard toward him. "Have a seat."

Darcie perched on the edge of a hard plastic chair and watched the man peck on the keyboard. It seemed an eternity later when he finally said, "You can go on back. Number three."

She'd left her purse in the car at Caleb's suggestion, so she passed through the metal detector with no delays. Caleb led her a short distance down a hallway, to an interior room with large windows, the glass reinforced with steel mesh. A row of booths lined the inside wall, each with a built-in computer monitor mounted above a narrow shelf that served as a miniature desk. A telephone sat on each shelf. Caleb led her to the booth that bore a large number three above the only monitor that was not black. She sat in the chair he held out for her. He grabbed a second chair and scooted it beside her. In the monitor she saw an empty chair, exactly like the ones in which they sat. Relief poured through her as she realized the manner of this visit.

"We're not going to be in the same room with him?"

Caleb shook his head. "We're not even in the same building. He's somewhere on the other side of the prison."

Why that should be such a relief, Darcie didn't know, but some of the tension that tied her stomach into knots relaxed.

A man slid into the chair in the monitor. Uncle Kenneth. She studied his face. The five years since she'd last seen him had not been kind. Heavy creases lined his skin, and the fuzz covering his nearly shaved head bore witness that the dark hair she remembered had faded to dull gray. His cheeks were hollow, giving him a haggard appearance. But the eyes were the same. They stared at some point below the monitor and narrowed slightly, as though studying something. Glancing upward, Darcie saw the circle of a lens mounted at the top of the screen and realized he was looking at her face in the monitor on his side.

His eyes slid sideways toward Caleb, and a question appeared on his brow. She saw his arm reach forward and then a telephone receiver appeared in his hand, which he held up to his ear. With a glance at Caleb, she picked up the phone on the shelf in front of her.

"Who's that?"

No greeting. No "It's good to see you," or "How have you been," just the same demanding tone from her memories.

Darcie glanced at Caleb. "A friend."

"What's he doing here?" He must have glanced upward at the camera, because for a moment it looked like his eyes met hers. "In fact, what are you doing here?"

"I need some help."

His lip curled. "Figured. You sure didn't decide to visit your only living relative out of the goodness of your heart."

Darcie tried to ignore the thinly veiled barb but couldn't. "Turns out you're not my only living relative after all. That's what I came to talk about."

A smile twisted the corners of his lips as he sat back in his chair. "So you finally found out, did you? What was it, your mother's deathbed confession?"

The reference to Mama's death, so casually mentioned, prodded at a tender place that she refused to let this man see. She didn't bother to answer the question. "I need to know about your relationship with my uncle Richard."

"Uncle Richard, is it?" He laughed. "Now that your mother's dead he's going to welcome you into the family fold, is he? Well, take a piece of advice from your *old* uncle." His expression hardened. "Don't trust that snake. Not for a minute. He'll throw you under a bus in a heartbeat if he thinks he'll make a dime off of you."

He obviously hadn't heard about Uncle Richard's death. She glanced at Caleb and then realized he couldn't hear. She leaned sideways and tilted the receiver outward so they could both listen. Caleb draped an arm over the back of her chair so he could draw closer and bent his ear toward the phone.

"I don't believe that," she said into the phone. "Uncle Richard cared about me and Mama far more than you ever did. He took care of us."

"Out of guilt." His free hand waved in a dismissive gesture. "And it didn't hurt him any, I guarantee that. What's a few thousand dollars twice a year compared to the millions he has? He sent Beth money to appease his own conscience, not out of any concern for you. Trust me, girl. If you're throwing your lot in with Fairmont because you think you might get some of his money, you're wrong."

The hand holding the receiver trembled with the urge to tell him how wrong he was. Caleb exerted a gentle pressure on her back with his hand and shook his head. She saw the wisdom of withholding the information about Uncle Richard's will. Kenneth would be released soon, and if he thought she had money, he would try to leech onto her as he had Mama.

Caleb's deep voice rumbled through his chest. "What is it between you and Fairmont? What do you have against him?"

At first she thought Kenneth might not answer. He turned a scowl on Caleb. But then he appeared to change his mind. "Besides the fact that I'm in this place because of him?"

Darcie wasn't about to let him get away with that. "You're in here because you stole from him."

He didn't bother to deny it. "He's a bigger thief than I ever was. But that's okay. When I get out of here I'll have the upper hand. He won't be able to touch me again. I've got some insurance tucked away right under his nose. A little security. And there's not a thing he can do about it."

What was he babbling about? Disgusted, she let the news out. "You don't have anything over him, not anymore. Uncle Richard was murdered last night."

The shock on his face gave her a momentary, and childish, sense of satisfaction. In the next instant it disappeared as Kenneth's surprise gave way to a smirk.

"Somebody finally got him, did they? Not surprised. He was prodding a hornet's nest five years ago. Apparently the hornets finally wised up."

"What do you mean?" Caleb asked.

But Kenneth refused to answer, just sat there shaking his head.

"Look, Pryor, whatever you know, we need to know, too. Fairmont's death wasn't the first. His wife's kennel manager was killed a couple of days before, right in his office not fifty yards from the house."

The image in the monitor straightened. "The kennel behind the pool house?"

"That's right."

"Mrs. Fairmont's still breeding those mutts, is she?"

Caleb's voice grew stern. "There's a murderer running around loose, and we've got to find him before he kills again."

Darcie could almost see the thoughts flying around in Kenneth's mind. She exchanged a glance with Caleb. That he was keeping a secret was obvious. The question was whether or not he would tell them.

With the return of the smirk, she knew the answer.

"I don't care how many people drop dead on Fairmont Estate. Good riddance."

"But what if I'm next?" Darcie demanded. "Don't you care about *your* only living relative?"

His head cocked sideways, and he stared at the screen. If only he would look up at the camera so she could see what was in his eyes.

"You stay away from that estate, you hear me? Far away."

She wished she could read a tiny bit of concern for her well-being in the warning. But who was she trying to fool? He hadn't given two shakes about her for almost twenty-two years. Why would he start now?

She stood, thrusting the telephone into Caleb's hands. "I'm through here."

Without waiting for an answer, and without another glance toward her uncle's image in the screen, she left the room. If that man was her only surviving blood relative, then she'd rather live the rest of her life alone.

FIFTEEN

For the first twenty minutes or so of the drive back to Atlanta, Darcie stared out the window, her expression troubled. Caleb left her alone with her thoughts and focused on reviewing the interview with Kenneth Pryor.

When she had stomped out of the room, Pryor wasn't interested in talking anymore. After a few unsuccessful attempts to get something new out of him, Caleb gave up and ended the visitation.

They were still an hour outside of Atlanta when she broke the silence. "Well, that was a waste of gas and time."

"You think so?"

"Don't you?"

He shrugged. "We didn't get anything solid, but at least we have a couple of things to think about."

She looked at him, her expression blank. "We do?"

"Sure. We verified that there's something more to the dislike between Pryor and Fairmont than the embezzlement. After five years, he still insists Fairmont is a crook."

"That's the way he justified his actions, by claiming that Uncle Richard was as big a thief as he is. As if that makes it all right." She showed her opinion of that idea with a disdainful toss of her head.

"Maybe, but I think there was more to his claims than that. I sure would like to know what he was talking about with that hornet's nest comment. It's almost like he was bragging, proud that he was going to beat a powerful man like Fairmont at his own game."

Questions rested in the face turned toward him. "So? That proves he's self-centered and delusional."

Caleb acknowledged that by dipping his head. "Maybe. Or maybe it's true."

Her chest puffed out. "That Uncle Richard was a thief? That's ridiculous. He's…he was a respected businessman. Politicians called him up to Washington for meetings, and he hosted fundraising dinners for them."

"So you're saying the fact that a bunch of Washington bureaucrats liked him proves he wasn't crooked?" He disarmed her with a grin, and her outrage gave way to a chuckle.

"*Touché.*" Then she sobered. "But that doesn't prove he was dishonest. And what was that babbling about insurance?"

"Exactly. That's something else for us to think about. What is the insurance Pryor mentioned?"

Her eyes unfocused as she considered the question. "Information of some kind? Proof, maybe, of

Uncle Richard's illegal activities?" She hurried to add, "Not that I believe that for a minute. If he had that kind of proof, why hasn't he told anyone before now?"

"I don't know," Caleb said, "but I don't think he was blowing smoke about that. He seemed genuinely pleased that he was going to be able to…how did he put it? Get the upper hand over Fairmont."

Reluctantly, Darcie nodded. "It did sound like bragging, didn't it? But I don't know how this can help us unless we find whatever it is he was talking about. We don't know what it is, much less where to look for it."

A mile passed with the only sound in the cab the wheels rumbling down the highway.

"You know what else was weird?" Caleb spoke slowly, thoughts falling into place as he said the words. "When I told him about Lewis being killed, his ears pricked up."

"You're right. But he couldn't have known Lewis, could he? Mrs. Fairmont said he'd only been her kennel manager a couple of years, and Uncle Kenneth has been in prison for five."

"That's what struck me as weird." Caleb pictured Pryor's face, the sudden flare of interest when he had mentioned Lewis. "He didn't ask anything about him, not even his name. He asked about the kennel."

"You're right," she said slowly. "He asked whether it was the kennel behind the pool house."

They looked at each other a minute, and then

Caleb said what they were both thinking. "Is his insurance hidden somewhere in the kennel?"

"Was the kennel even there five years ago?" she asked. "The building didn't look very old. It certainly wasn't part of the original estate."

Caleb grinned. It would probably lead to nothing, but at least it was a trail to follow. He leaned down to grab his cell phone from the cup holder and handed it to her.

"Call Mason. Number two on speed dial. Ask him if he can find out when that kennel was built."

"Bingo."

Mason marched into the Emersons' kitchen the next day while Darcie and Caleb were finishing up a sandwich for lunch. Lauren had returned to work after taking a few days off. Darcie suspected she and the others had made a pact of some kind not to leave her alone, because her hostess didn't leave for work until after Caleb had arrived that morning. She didn't ask, though. Having the big man around gave her a sense of security she needed right now.

Mason set his backpack on the floor, dropped into an empty chair and slapped a file folder on the table. "The building permit for the construction of a kennel on Fairmont Estate was issued in January five years ago." He flipped open the folder, pulled out a copy of a sketch and slid it across the table toward Caleb. "That was three months before Pryor's arrest."

Darcie positioned the sketch so both she and Caleb

could see it. Rectangles and squares with dozens of crisscrossing lines and handwritten measurements meant nothing to her, though the long rectangle probably represented the kennel building.

Caleb apparently had no trouble interpreting the foreign-looking diagram. "Looks like they made some changes to the pool house at the same time."

"Yeah, some heavy-duty remodeling. Added that office and attached the two buildings with a breezeway." Mason shoved the folder forward. "Details are all in there."

While Caleb opened the folder and flipped through the papers inside, Mason made no attempt to hide the longing with which he stared at the half-eaten sandwich on Darcie's plate.

"Would you like a sandwich?" she asked.

He brightened. "Love it. I was too busy researching building projects to eat."

She left the table and headed for the refrigerator. "So that means Uncle Kenneth was still employed by Uncle Richard when construction started on the kennel. He could have hidden something in there."

Caleb wore a troubled expression. "I don't buy it. Where could he put it that someone wouldn't find it in five years?"

"What *it* are we talking about?" Mason asked.

"I wish I knew." Caleb scratched his chin absently and flipped a page over.

"It could be anything," Darcie said. "Maybe he hid it inside a wall or something."

"If so, we'll never find it. That kennel is six hundred square feet with six interior walls. That's a lot of wall space. And I doubt Mrs. Fairmont would be too happy with us knocking walls open to look."

She took a plate from the cabinet and assembled a sandwich of thickly sliced ham, Swiss cheese and rye bread. Percy left the corner where his bed had been located to sit hopefully on the floor at Mason's side when she placed the sandwich on the table in front of him. Mason closed his eyes for a quick silent prayer, and then attacked his lunch in much the same way Percy devoured his breakfast every morning.

"I know one of the inspectors." Caleb tapped a scrawled signature on one of the papers. "I've worked with him a couple of times. Maybe I'll give him a call and see what he remembers about that job."

What good that would do, Darcie couldn't imagine. But at least it was something.

Percy, having realized Mason was not planning to share his lunch, returned to his bed.

Caleb's eyes followed the dog. "How long has Mrs. Fairmont been breeding dogs?"

Darcie tried to follow his train of thought. "Obviously more than five years, because Kenneth mentioned it. He asked if she was still breeding her dogs."

"He called them her mutts." Caleb gazed at her with a teasing grin.

"Which shows his ignorance. Those dogs cost over a thousand dollars each."

Disbelief colored his face. "For a dog so small it would get lost in one of my boots?" He examined Percy again.

Mason spoke around a mouthful of sandwich. "I like dogs, but that's insane."

Even Darcie had to agree. "When Percy was first delivered to our house I looked up Fairmont Designer Dogs on the internet. Mrs. Fairmont doesn't have a website or anything, but she does put notices on places like PuppyFind.com when she has puppies for sale. The notice I saw said clearly that prospective owners would be interviewed to ensure a suitable placement."

Both men looked at her as if she were crazy.

"You mean I'd have to go through an interview before I was *allowed* to fork over a thousand bucks for a dog?" Caleb shook his head slowly. "That's nuts. If I wanted a dog, I'd head down to the pound."

"You can't find a dog like Percy at the Humane Society."

The moment the words left her mouth, she realized they weren't true. Sloane and her mother had found their puppy at the pound. That pup looked enough like Percy to be a littermate.

Caleb remembered. "I'll bet your neighbor didn't pay that much for her pup."

"Yes, but Purdy didn't come with the collar," Darcie said.

He looked blank. "Collar?"

"That's right. It's actually a brilliant marketing idea. Every Fairmont Designer Dog comes with a jeweled collar. It's what makes them worth so much more than other Maltipom puppies. In dog circles those collars are a mark of prestige."

Mason let out a disgusted grunt. "So people can brag about handing over a thousand bucks to someone who already has more money than she knows what to do with. That's just wrong."

"Actually, the money goes to charity," Darcie told him. "That's another thing I read on that notice. So people can feel good about spending the money for a designer dog because they're actually making a contribution to charity."

"And Fairmont gets the tax write-off." Caleb gave a grudging smile. "Pretty smart. For Fairmont, that is, but I still say it's stupid to spend so much on a dog when you can get the same thing at the pound."

His comment stuck in Darcie's mind. Something about Sloane's dog bothered her. If Purdy really was a Maltipom, what was she doing at the Humane Society? Nobody in their right mind would pay a thousand dollars for a dog and then leave it at the pound. Did the owner pass away maybe? Percy might have been taken to the pound after Mama died if she'd had no relatives who wanted him.

"About that collar." Caleb's voice was thoughtful. "Do you still have it?"

Darcie saw where he was going. "Yes, but trust me, it's not worth anything. I'll show you."

She scooted her chair out and headed upstairs to get Mama's shoe box. When she returned, Mason had taken a laptop out of his backpack and was powering up.

"It's really gaudy." She pulled it out of the box and handed it to Caleb. "There's no way I'd ever put that thing on Percy."

Every inch of the collar was covered with green-and-clear rhinestones in silver-plated settings. From the front hung a jeweled charm in the shape of a Saint Bernard's barrel.

"It's way too big for a dog the size of a loaf of bread." Caleb hefted the thing in his hand. "And too heavy as well."

She agreed with a nod. "The only thing it's good for is bragging rights, and I don't know anybody who'd be impressed."

He turned the collar in his hand, examining it from all angles. "You don't suppose these jewels are real, do you?"

Darcie's first instinct was to laugh. What an absurd idea. But then again, her apartment had been searched. Her car had been broken into. What if the thief hadn't been looking for the letters after all?

"Here, lemme see." Mason held out a hand. When Caleb gave him the collar, he held it up to the light. "Definitely not. The green ones are too cloudy to be emeralds, and those diamonds aren't even CZ. They're plain old rhinestones."

"How do you know that?" she asked.

His face took on a look of mock self-importance. "I have a wealth of knowledge about a wide variety of things."

Caleb blew a raspberry as Darcie took the collar from him and returned it to the box.

Mason pointed at his computer screen. "I found a newspaper article from last fall about Fairmont Designer Dogs." His eyes moved as he scanned the monitor. "They interviewed Jason Lewis, and he talks about the collars and the money going to charity. They also interviewed someone who bought one of the thousand-dollar dogs. Listen to this. 'Mrs. Cordelia Gates of Ansley Park recently bought two Fairmont Designer Dogs. "I love my babies," says Mrs. Gates. "They're my only family, and I pamper them shamelessly."'" Mason rolled his eyes.

"I know her," Caleb commented. "I did some work for her last year restoring her house."

Darcie grinned at him. "Mason knows everything, and you know everybody. What does Brent know?"

"Computers," he answered without hesitation. "He can do anything with a computer."

"Here you go, Caleb." Mason grinned over the top of the screen. "Fairmont Designer Dogs has puppies for sale right now. Says they'll be ready to go on June 12, and they're taking applications. I think you should fill one out."

"Right." He glanced over at Percy. "No offense, mutt, but that ain't happening."

When they'd gotten Percy he'd been twelve weeks old. The puppies she saw at the Fairmont Kennel looked close to the same size he'd been then. Actually, Sloan's puppy wasn't much bigger than those pups.

"Do me a favor," she said to Mason. "Search for Maltipom and Humane Society."

His fingers tapped, and he stared at the monitor. "Yep. Quite a few hits, in fact. There are Maltipoms on the websites of shelters in Arlington, Virginia, North Carolina, Vermont." He shook his head. "There's even one out in Utah."

Darcie left her chair to go stand beside him. "Do they have pictures?"

"Let's see."

Caleb joined them as he clicked on the first link. The screen opened up to display the picture of a fluffy white face with black button eyes.

"It could be Percy," Caleb commented.

Darcie studied the photo. Something strange was going on. "You know, most Maltipoms aren't solid white like Percy. It depends on their parents' coloring. But that's another of the trademarks of Fairmont Designer Dogs—they're all white. Let's look at another one."

Of the eight Humane Society websites that listed Maltipoms, only two showed pictures of dogs with brown markings. The rest were solid white, including two in the DC area. And they looked young, just puppies.

Darcie returned to her chair, her thoughts whirling. How could six Fairmont dogs end up in animal shelters? Of course, they might not be Fairmont dogs. But they certainly did look like Percy and Purdy.

Caleb also wore a thoughtful expression. "One in Arlington and two in DC where Mr. Fairmont was earlier this week. Makes me wonder if somebody ought to catch a flight up there and check them out."

She shook her head. "It probably wouldn't do any good. Puppies get adopted quickly, especially small breeds."

His head cocked sideways. "How do you know that?"

She couldn't hold back a grin. "You know people. I know dogs."

Mason pulled out his cell phone. "Let's call these shelters. Who knows? We might learn something."

They each made two calls. As Darcie suspected, all of the puppies had been adopted quickly. Every one had been dropped off anonymously, and none of them had collars.

Caleb cocked his head and stared at Percy. "I want to see another of these expensive pooches."

"What for?" Mason asked.

The big man shrugged. "We've got nothing else."

"We could go back to my apartment and look at Purdy," Darcie said, but he shook his head.

"No, I want to see one we know came from Mrs.

Fairmont. And I want to get a look at another collar, too. I'm going to give Mrs. Gates a call."

Frustration churned in Darcie's belly. What good would looking at another Maltipom be? But Caleb was right. The only other thing they had come up with was the possibility of something being hidden in the kennel building, and what could they do with that? Sneak onto Fairmont Estate and search? They'd be arrested for trespassing. Call Samuels? She shuddered. Not only would he be furious that they'd visited Kenneth in prison; he'd say their suspicions were nothing but a hunch. And he'd be right.

She swallowed her frustration and collected the empty lunch plates from the table while Caleb punched a number into his cell phone. It would be so easy to relax here in the safety of Lauren and Brent's house. If she tried, she might even be able to forget about death and school and worrying over her plans for the future.

Then she remembered the pressure of the kidnapper's hand clamped over her mouth and the terror of being pulled backward toward the dark interior of the van. Had her attackers given up on finding her? Or were they still out there, waiting to catch her unawares?

SIXTEEN

Mrs. Gates couldn't see them until that evening, and Caleb's call to his building inspector buddy went unanswered. He left a message.

A jittery feeling had settled on him after Mason left, and he circled the house a dozen times, checking locks and looking out windows. He saw nothing suspicious but couldn't shake the feeling that something was wrong.

What is it? What am I missing?

No matter how hard he tried, he couldn't come up with anything.

Darcie had settled in a chair in the family room with the dog in her lap. The television set was tuned to some shopping show to which she paid no attention. Every time Caleb looked in on her, she was staring off into space, her expression pensive. He considered taking control of the remote and trying to lose himself in a John Wayne movie, but he rejected the idea. In a weird way, watching television with a girl seemed a little too familiar. Best keep to the other room and to his plan to remain emotionally distant from Darcie Wiley. As distant as possible, anyway, while fulfilling his promise to protect her.

When his cell phone rang, he dashed from the front living room window to the kitchen and snatched it off the table.

"Hello?"

Noise filled the line. It took him a moment to identify the loud whine of a power saw and what might be a commercial truck beeping in reverse.

"Hey, Buchanan, this is John Taylor." The voice shouted over the noise. "Got your message. What's up?"

The building inspector. "Hey, brother. Thanks for calling me back." He paced to the patio door and stared into the backyard as he talked. "You got a minute? I need to ask you about a job you inspected a few years back."

"A few *years*?" Taylor barked a laugh. "Do you know how many buildings I inspect? I barely remember what I saw a few weeks ago."

"Yeah, I know what you mean, but I gotta ask. Maybe when you have a minute you could check your files or something. It was construction of a kennel on Richard Fairmont's property."

During the pause that followed. Darcie appeared in the kitchen doorway. She wrapped her arms around her middle and leaned against the doorjamb, watching him.

"Hold on," Taylor said. "Let me get someplace where I can talk."

What was that in his voice? Hesitancy? Or caution? Caleb waited, and then with a bang the noise went silent.

"There. I'm sitting in my truck. Now, why in the world are you asking about Fairmont's kennel?"

Caleb would prefer not to explain. The fewer people who knew that he was poking around in the Fairmonts' business, the better. He answered vaguely. "Oh, just something I'm checking out for a friend. No big deal."

"Yeah?" Taylor's voice became suspicious. "Pardon me if I don't buy that, especially not after a murder happened at the kennel a few days ago, and then Fairmont himself was found dead in his office. This wouldn't happen to have anything to do with those deaths, does it?"

He blew out a breath. Dumb not to have foreseen that Taylor would know about all that. Both deaths had been all over the news. "Maybe."

Silence. And then, "What do you want to know?"

"Well, that's the problem. I'm not sure. Do you remember the job?"

"Oh yeah. I won't ever forget that one."

Caleb straightened to attention, his gaze locked on Darcie's. "Why not?"

Taylor's voice lowered. "Because that was the first time I was ever offered a bribe to falsify a record."

Excitement prickled the hair along the back of Caleb's scalp. "What record were you asked to falsify?"

Darcie's eyes widened, and she took a step closer.

"Routine inspections," he replied. "The first time I went out there they'd poured the slab for the kennel building. Everything looked fine. But then they called for the second inspection, I was on my way out there when Doug Norville called. He was one of the senior managers down at the Community Development Department. He told me he had it covered."

"Is that unusual?"

"Oh yeah." He gave a short laugh. "Once those guys work their way up into management, most of them wouldn't be caught dead dirtying their hands on a job site. Especially a dog kennel."

While he spoke, Caleb flipped open the file folder on the kitchen table and paged through the papers with his free hand until he found copies of the building inspections. Sure enough, Taylor had only signed the first one.

"It was probably a big deal since the kennel belonged to Mrs. Fairmont," Caleb said.

"That's what I figured—Norville wanted to rub elbows with the rich people. And hey, what did I care? Let him. But when I was heading out to my afternoon job I had to drive right past the Fairmont place, so I stopped in. I admit I was curious to see if the guy was going to do a real inspection or just a cursory walk-through so he could schmooze with the Fairmonts."

The scrawled signature on the subsequent inspection reports was nothing more than a squiggly line, completely unreadable. The first letter might have been a *D*. "Was he there?"

"Oh yeah. Talking to the job foreman. But I knew as soon as I walked around the pool building that something fishy was going on. They weren't only building a kennel."

Caleb flipped over to the sketch. "I have a copy of the sketch in front of me. Looks like they also added a good-size room on to the existing pool house and connected it to the kennel with a breezeway."

"Yeah, that's what it looked like on the sketch they filed, and that's what was approved by the department. But that isn't all they did."

Caleb tightened his grip on the cell phone. This was it, something big. He could feel it. "What was going on there?"

Taylor's voice dropped to little more than a whisper. "That extra room they added to the pool house? They also dug an underground room right beneath it."

"A secret room?"

Darcie's mouth fell open.

"That's right. And it's not on any of the building records. You should have seen Norville's face when he saw me come around the corner of that building. He scooted me out of there so quick I barely got a look at it, but there's no hiding a twenty-by-twenty hole in the ground."

"What did he say about it?"

"He gave me a long explanation about how Fairmont wanted an underground place for his safe and other valuables, and how rich people install places like that all the time and it doesn't show up on any building plans because then it would be a matter of public record."

"And he offered you a bribe to keep your mouth shut?"

"First he told me he wanted me to sign the inspection report." He sounded offended. "I told him there was no way I was going to sign my name to a false inspection, and he insisted that he'd just finished the inspection and everything was up to code. He didn't come right out and offer me cash, but he hinted at it. Told me Mr. Fairmont was a powerful man who could afford to pay well to make sure his privacy was respected. Well, that ticked me off, so I told him he could sign the report himself but I wasn't having anything to do with it."

Caleb tapped on the illegible signature. "Apparently that's what he did."

"So I understand. When I left that place he *advised* me—" he drew the word out with a sarcastic drawl "—to forget everything I'd seen and that's what I did. Never even pulled the file to see what happened. I figured with a name as big as Fairmont's, it was in my best interest to steer clear and keep my mouth shut."

"What is he saying?" Darcie whispered.

Caleb mouthed, *I'll tell you in a minute.* To Taylor he said, "Sounds like a good decision. Especially now."

It took a second before his meaning became clear to Taylor. "Do you think that underground room has something to do with the murders? I looked up all the news reports on the internet and not one of them mentioned a secret room, or anything stolen either. They said the kennel manager's body was found in his office and Fairmont was found in his."

"That's true." Caleb knew that for a fact, but who knew what else the police had found after he and Darcie left? Certainly Samuels didn't mention an underground room. The surly detective wasn't exactly forthcoming with information, though. Still, he should be told, just in case it had any bearing on his investigation.

"That room probably has nothing to do with the deaths," he told Taylor, "but maybe you ought to call the police."

"Me? No way."

"Why not? I can give you the direct phone number of the investigating detective."

A frustrated breath blew into Caleb's ear. "Do you know where Doug Norville is now, Buchanan? He's the senior director over the whole department. My boss's boss's boss."

"Apparently doing a favor to a rich guy like Fairmont was good for his career," Caleb commented drily.

A bitter laugh answered him. "Yeah, and I'm still a lowly building inspector, but I need this job. If all goes well I'm up for early retirement in three more years, and I'm counting the days. So do me a favor, will you?"

Caleb knew what he was going to say. "Don't tell the police anything we just discussed."

"Yeah." He sounded sheepish. "Not unless you find out that the room might be important. And even then, could you not tell them where you heard about it?"

Caleb hesitated. Darcie watched him closely, her fingers biting into the fleshy part of her arms. Eventually Samuels would discover that secret room, and if he found out Caleb had known about it, he might just carry through on his threat to arrest him for obstruction. On the other hand, if Caleb confessed that he'd made a few calls, Samuels would arrest him for obstruction *now* rather than later. Then who would get to the bottom of these murders and the attack on Darcie?

"All right," he told Taylor. "You have my word."

"Thanks." He sounded relieved.

They hung up after promising to get together sometime soon for a burger, and then Caleb relayed the details of the conversation to Darcie.

"What do you think Uncle Richard had in that room?" she asked.

"I don't know, piles of money maybe?" He shrugged. "What I'd like to know is whether or not Pryor knew about the room."

"Uncle Kenneth?" A moment later understanding

dawned on her face. "You think he might have hidden his mysterious insurance down there?"

"It's possible." He flipped through the papers in the folder until he found the first inspection record. "My buddy signed this on April third. Do you remember when Pryor was arrested?"

Her nose scrunched as she considered. "It was sometime in May, I think. I remember it was the end of the school year. We could probably find out the exact date if you think it's important. There are bound to be records."

Caleb turned that page over and looked at the next one. "The next inspection occurred on May twenty-eighth. Taylor said he saw a twenty-foot hole in the ground that day."

"Since Kenneth was employed by Uncle Richard right up until his arrest, he could have known about the secret room."

"And hidden something there?" He shook his head. "In order to make sure no one else found it, it would have to be inside the concrete walls. How could he retrieve it?"

They had no answers to their questions. Only Pryor knew what he was talking about, and after the prison visit Caleb knew asking would be a waste of breath.

It's time to forget about Pryor's insurance, focus on something else. It's a dead-end trail.

Was that the Lord's nudge or his own frustration speaking? The answer was profoundly disturbing.

Caleb had no idea. Which meant he could no longer tell the difference. Either he had become so self-deluded that he couldn't hear the Lord anymore or God had stopped talking to him.

Storm clouds had filled the sky by the time Darcie followed Caleb down the curved walkway of a beautiful early 1900s home in the affluent Ansley Park neighborhood. From somewhere above them the sun tried to shine through with little effect. The sky was a mass of dark, threatening clouds that threw Mrs. Gates's lush green lawn into shadows.

"What did you tell her on the phone?" she asked Caleb as they mounted the steps to a wide-columned porch.

"I told her we were looking at a Fairmont puppy and were interested in seeing one that's matured a bit."

Darcie arched her brows in a mock reprimand. "You mean you lied?"

Caleb looked offended. "I did not lie. We *were* looking at a puppy the other day—several of them, in fact. And we are interested in seeing hers, which are more mature."

She tilted her head to bestow a skeptical look and had the satisfaction of seeing his cheeks redden.

"Okay, so I used a few carefully worded phrases to avoid telling her the real reason. I don't want to drag a nice lady like Mrs. Gates into what might become a dangerous situation. The less she knows, the better."

"Hey, you don't have to explain anything to me. I understand." She really did. And yet Darcie found herself the slightest bit disappointed in the big man. Wasn't a twisted word the same thing as an outright lie? Maybe not exactly, but both were deceitful, something she hadn't thought Caleb capable of.

He rang the bell and immediately a familiar sound came from inside the house—the enthusiastic high-pitched bark from not one, but two canine throats. The door edged open a crack, and the barking increased to a frantic speed.

"Now, Lance, behave yourself." A deep female voice held a tone of indulgence thinly disguised as a scold. "This is a friend, not a salesman. Look how good Gwen is being. Here. Come to Mother."

The door opened to reveal a stout woman with a tolerant smile for the dog she cradled in one arm. "Don't worry," she told Caleb. "He sounds ferocious, but he's really something of a grandstander, all bluster and show." Her gaze lowered and fixed on Darcie, and she continued in an amused tone, "He's very much like my late husband in that respect. I learned to let Paul blather as much as he liked. It made him feel important."

Darcie couldn't stop a grin. She liked this woman already.

Mrs. Gates's head tilted as she looked up at her visitor. "Caleb, I'd forgotten how tall you are. My goodness, you should have taken up basketball. Well, don't stand there on the porch. Come in. Duck your head, I don't want to be responsible for a concussion."

She stepped back and gestured them inside. Caleb caught Darcie's eye and smiled as he indicated that she should precede him into the house. That he felt comfortable in this woman's presence was obvious. Darcie herself felt some of the tension seep out of her muscles as she entered the house.

When the door closed, Mrs. Gates set the dog on the floor beside another one, both so like Percy that she would be hard put to tell the three apart if she saw them separately.

"These are my babies." Pride swelled the woman's voice and her ample bosom. "Lancelot and Guinevere."

Darcie squatted down on her haunches and held a hand out for their inspection. Side by side as they were now, she saw that Lancelot stood a tad taller than Guinevere, who sniffed at Darcie's hand experimentally, definitely the more cautious of the two. Lancelot had no reservations about how to greet a stranger. He leaped toward Darcie, but instead of stopping at her hand, hopped on his hind legs to bathe her face with an enthusiastic tongue.

Mrs. Gates swooped him up in her arms again. "And yet another trait he shares with Paul. He loves the ladies." She tucked the dog into the crook of one arm and thrust her hand toward Darcie. "Especially pretty ones like you, my dear. I am Cordelia Gates. And you are…"

Caleb supplied the introduction. "This is my friend, Darcie Wiley."

"It's nice to meet you, Mrs. Gates." She took the proffered hand and found hers captured in a surprisingly firm grip.

"Call me Cordelia. I don't stand on ceremony." Instead of releasing Darcie's hand, Cordelia pulled her down a hallway. "When you called this morning, I asked my housekeeper if she would make us a snack to enjoy while you visit. It's right in here."

"We can't stay," Caleb protested, falling in behind them. "We only wanted to take a look at your dogs."

"Oh, it's not much. Don't worry, I won't keep you long."

They entered a cheerfully cluttered kitchen, and Darcie found herself tugged toward a sturdy round table laden with so much food the bowls and platters crowded the three place settings.

"Not much food?" She eyed the table and then turned an incredulous look on Caleb. "Look at all this."

A variety of finger sandwiches filled a tiered serving tray beside a bowl filled with a colorful berry salad. An artistic arrangement of crackers surrounded a wedge of Brie on a platter next to a sectioned tray that boasted an assortment of fresh vegetables. In the center of the table stood a layer cake with sliced strawberries atop fluffy white icing.

"We should have brought Mason," Caleb said.

Cordelia bent over to set Lancelot on the floor and then bustled toward the refrigerator. "My new housekeeper is something of an overachiever, which is one reason I love her. Now, have a seat while I pour the iced tea, and then we'll talk."

Cordelia refused to let them ask a single question before they'd filled their plates. When Darcie took only one petite sandwich, she piled three more on her plate because, "They're small, so it takes four to make one."

When she had offered a brief blessing, she picked up the cheese knife and sliced off a generous portion of Brie. "Now, which of you is getting a puppy?"

Darcie's gaze slid sideways to Caleb. How would he answer?

He kept his eyes on his plate. "To be honest, I'm not sure I really want a dog. But I know Mrs. Fairmont has puppies that are almost ready to go. Darcie has one, and she's been happy with him." He speared a piece of melon with a fork, still avoiding the older woman's eye. "If I *were* going to get a dog, that seems like a good breed to have."

A carefully worded answer.

Cordelia beamed at Darcie. "You have a Maltipom? Oh, my dear, aren't they delightful?" She turned an indulgent smile on her two furry babies, who were jumping on their hind legs beside her chair. She broke off two bits of sandwich and fed the beggars.

"Yes, ma'am, they are. And smart, too."

"Oh yes." She nodded, then flashed a dimple across the table. "My two have me perfectly trained to spoil them rotten." As if to prove her point, she fed them each a cracker spread with Brie.

"How did you settle on this kind of dog?" Caleb asked. "Do you know Mrs. Fairmont?"

"Oh, no. I don't run in the same circles as Olivia. She's a very nice person and I admire her for her charity patronage, but her lifestyle is far too lofty for my blood. Or my pocketbook. No, I chose my darlings for their size and temperament." A twinkle sparked in her eyes. "And for the collars, of course."

"Have you ever put the collars on them?" Darcie asked.

"Those hideous things? Of course not. Lance and Gwen would think I was cross with them if I strapped those heavy things around their necks. No, I keep them on display in the living room so my bridge club ladies can enjoy them when they come." A smirk hovered around her lips.

Caleb leaned forward over his plate. "Could we see them?"

"Of course." She left the table, both dogs trotting after her, and returned with two jeweled collars. "This is Guenivere's." She handed one to Darcie and the other to Caleb. "And this is Lancelot's."

Darcie turned the collar over in her hand. It was the same bulky size as Percy's, but instead of green stones this one had pink. The pattern of the silver settings was a little different, too, and the charm that swung from the clasp was in the shape of a rhinestone-covered heart. While Cordelia returned to her chair, Darcie traded with Caleb. Lance's collar bore imitation blue sapphires, and, instead of a dangling charm, a jewel-encrusted bow tie was attached to the center.

Darcie handed the blue one across the table. "Percy's is similar, but the stones are green and the charm is bulkier. It's in the shape of one of those Saint Bernard barrels."

"Oh, every Fairmont collar is unique." Caleb handed her the pink one, and she held them up to one another. "That's what makes them special." She beamed down at her babies and continued in the baby talk used by overly indulgent dog owners. "Just wike you are special, isn't that wight, widdle ones?"

Caleb's eyes rolled upward, and Darcie turned her head to hide a smile. Mama had used the same baby talk with Percy.

Cordelia took another sandwich from the tray and divided it into two. As far as Darcie could tell, she had yet to put a bite in her own mouth, but the dogs were certainly enjoying the "snack."

"Regardless of the collars," the woman told Caleb, "Maltipoms are perfectly delightful dogs. Smart, and they don't shed as much as other dogs. And the Fairmont dogs have such wonderful personalities. If you are serious about adding a puppy to your family, I highly recommend them." She reached across the table and patted his arm, affection shining in her eyes. "And you would be such a good dog parent, dear. Someone as sweet as you deserves a puppy to brighten your life."

A guilty flush crept up Caleb's neck. He stole a quick glance at Darcie, who refused to feel sorry for him.

He should *feel guilty for deceiving a sweet lady like her.*

He surprised her by hanging his head, his shoulders slumped. "Mrs. Gates, I have a confession. I'm not planning to buy a puppy."

Well, what do you know? He couldn't keep up the deception. For some reason, his commitment to honesty made her feel better.

"You're not?" Cordelia's voice displayed dismay. But then she looked across the table and winked privately at Darcie. "Then why did you want to visit my babies, Caleb?"

Darcie scooped up her napkin and made a show of wiping her mouth so Caleb wouldn't see her smile. Cordelia hadn't been fooled for a second.

"If you don't mind, I'd rather not say, ma'am," he told her miserably.

She lifted her tea glass and brought it to her lips. "Would the reason have anything to do with the death of that poor man at the kennel the other day and then Richard Fairmont's so soon after?"

Caleb's head jerked toward her.

She sipped her tea and then calmly returned the

glass to the table. "My dear, just because I'm old doesn't mean I'm naive. I watch the news. And besides, you and I talked quite a bit while you were remodeling my upstairs bathroom. I remember how you dislike dogs." She shook her head sadly in Darcie's direction. "A flaw in an otherwise admirable character, if you ask me."

Caleb's breath heaved. "I'm sorry. I didn't want to involve you in what might be a dangerous situation."

"Dangerous? Oh, dear." Spots of pink appeared on her cheeks, and her eyes sparkled with excitement. "Whatever have you two gotten yourselves into?" She leaned eagerly over her plate, waiting for an answer.

"We don't know," Darcie answered honestly. "But we're beginning to wonder if those murders have something to do with the Fairmont dogs."

"A natural assumption, since the first victim was found at the kennel." She plucked a grape off of her plate and popped it into her mouth. "I met that Mr. Lewis, you know. He took my application for my darlings and, when I was approved, let me spend as much time as I wanted selecting them from among their littermates. It wasn't until I arrived to pick them up weeks later that I finally met Olivia."

"What was he like?" Caleb asked.

Her lips pursed into a prim bow. "I know one shouldn't speak ill of the dead, but I wasn't fond of him. Oh, he knew his business about dogs, mind you. Still, something about him reminded me of my husband's brother Lionel. Secretive. I always suspected Lionel of hiding something. Paul used to tell me I was imagining things, until the police showed up at Lionel's house and arrested him for theft. They found an entire dresser drawer full of stolen wristwatches. There were even two of Paul's." She clucked her tongue and then reached for a grape. "I wonder if the police searched Mr. Lewis's dresser drawers."

"Did you know Mr. Fairmont?" asked Caleb.

She shook her head. "I never had the opportunity to meet him. But Olivia is a lovely woman, don't you think?"

Darcie held her tongue while Caleb mumbled something noncommittal.

The rest of the meal passed pleasantly enough. Darcie let Cordelia's chatter lull her into believing, if only for a few minutes, that this was a perfectly normal meal with a charming and talkative host and a pair of spoiled dogs. All too soon it was time to go. As she followed Caleb out of the cheerful clutter of Cordelia's home, Darcie felt like she was being thrown out of a shelter and back into a raging storm.

Almost literally. The clouds overhead had darkened even further, and the air held the heavy scent of impending rain.

Cordelia walked them to the edge of the porch and leaned over to cast an apprehensive look up at the sky. "Oh, dear. This might be a bad one. Still, we need the rain." She hugged Guinevere close. "Be careful, you two."

"We will," Darcie promised as Caleb opened the truck door.

The older woman's solemn expression deepened. "I don't mean with the weather, dear."

A weight sank in the pit of Darcie's stomach as she nodded. "Yes, ma'am. I know."

She climbed into the truck as the first fat raindrops splattered against the windshield. Caleb hurried around the front and slid into his seat.

"Thank you," he called out the window, then turned the ignition key. The engine thrummed to life.

As the truck backed down the driveway Cordelia lifted one of Guinevere's fuzzy paws and waved goodbye. With another upward glance, she quickstepped up the walk toward the house. She had barely reached the shelter of her porch when the heavens opened.

Darcie quickly rolled the window up. Within seconds the woman and her dog were lost to sight behind a gray curtain of water.

The truck plunged forward, headlights slicing through the rain. "I'd forgotten what a sharp cookie she is," Caleb said.

"I like her a lot." Darcie tilted her head to look at his profile. "What made you decide to be honest with her?"

His lungs deflated with a breath. "I couldn't keep

on twisting words and look her in the face. I like her, too. I just hope we haven't gotten her into any trouble."

"I don't see how. She didn't tell us anything."

Caleb agreed. "I don't know what I was hoping to find, but that was a dead end for sure. I think she enjoyed our visit, though. And her dogs enjoyed themselves, what with all the sandwiches and cheese."

"I did find out something I've wondered about." She leaned over and lifted the shoe box at her feet to the bench between them, then took out Percy's collar. "All the collars are just as gaudy as this one. In the back of my mind I'd kind of wondered if ours was the only ugly one." She looked at the collar. "Although I liked that little bow tie much better than this bulky barrel."

In the next moment the truck lurched sideways. The back tires swerved as Caleb executed a quick right turn onto the interstate on-ramp.

Alarmed, she grabbed on to the door handle and looked at Caleb. "What was that?"

"Sorry." His lips pressed into a tight line, both hands gripping the steering wheel. "I was checking something."

Irritation made her voice snap. "What, like how much I can take before I lose my supper?"

"No, like whether or not that car back there is following us." He glanced into the rearview mirror, and his expression turned grim. "Looks like our friends from the other night have caught up with us again."

SEVENTEEN

The onslaught of this much rain would have made visibility difficult in the best of circumstances. Caleb clutched the steering wheel in a white-knuckled grip and strained his eyes for the white lines that defined the road. A line of red taillights from cars that had pulled off the interstate to wait for a lull in the storm sped by in a blurry glare. In the rearview mirror twin circles of light told him their tail was riding close. If he tapped his brakes, the car might even kiss his bumper. In weather like this, that could end in disaster.

Darcie twisted around in her seat to look through the back window. "What are they doing? Are they trying to cause a wreck?"

Caleb didn't answer. The same thought had occurred to him, and he didn't like the implication.

They hit a deep puddle in the road, and water slammed into the pickup's frame with a sound like an explosion. The pickup's rear end fishtailed. A frightened scream came from Darcie's side of the cab, but Caleb barely had time to notice. He took his foot off the accelerator and counter-steered. With a jolt the rear tires caught traction and righted. The truck jumped forward.

The car stayed its course, barely two feet behind him.

"Any sign of a police car?" Darcie's voice trembled as she stared forward through eyes round as hubcaps.

"Not yet."

He didn't say so, but he doubted the same ploy would work on this stretch of interstate. They'd be fortunate to pass a cruiser pulled off to wait out the storm. But if those were the same guys as before, they'd be wise to that trick. Besides, they were acting differently this time. No attempt to mask their presence. Instead, they were in open and aggressive pursuit.

Which could only mean one thing.

"Darcie, I want you to do something for me." He spoke as calmly as he could, but his insides were as taut as guitar strings. "Bend over and bury your face in your knees. Put both hands over your head."

A frightened sob answered him, but in his peripheral vision he watched her obey. Not a moment too soon.

He'd traveled this part of the interstate often when he had worked on Mrs. Gates house last year. They were quickly approaching a left curve with a steep embankment on the right. If he was correct, the car behind them would—

The truck jerked as the car's bumper slammed into them. A muffled cry came from Darcie's doubled-over body. Caleb fought to keep the steering wheel steady. The car rammed them again, and the rear end skidded sideways. He jerked the wheel to steer into the skid, but this time the tires found no purchase on the wet road. The front of the truck swung around and—

"Hang on," he shouted. "We're going over."

The next few seconds were a blur. He was thrown sideways and his head connected with the window. Instinct kicked in and his hands left the wheel to cover his face. Darcie's screams echoed inside the cab and were abruptly cut off. He barely had time to worry about that when he felt cold water pelting his upper body. All the while the world rocked and jerked and whirled.

And then came to an abrupt halt.

Dazed, Caleb didn't move for a moment. His brain struggled to throw off a numbing shock. Pain throbbed in his left thigh. Not broken-bone pain, thank the Lord, more like someone had whopped him with a two-by-four. His neck ached and his elbow burned. Gingerly, he flexed his toes, moved his knees slightly, shrugged his shoulders. Everything appeared to be in working order.

A noise punched through his mental inventory and it took him a second to place it. Someone crying. He jerked upright and ignored the stab of pain in his thigh the sudden movement caused.

"Darcie!"

His vision blurred, and for a panicked moment he thought he'd been blinded. Then he realized rain was pouring onto his face through the empty place where the windshield had been, and he wiped his eyes with his hand.

The passenger side of the cab had been mangled. The roof looked like a tree had fallen on it and the metal had crumpled like tinfoil. Darcie was tucked beneath it, still doubled over, as though she'd taken shelter from the storm in a crushed metal cave.

Caleb fumbled with his seat belt clasp. "Darcie, are you hurt?"

Relief poured over him like the rain when her muffled voice replied, "I don't think so. Not badly, anyway. But this is really uncomfortable."

Relief transformed tension to laughter, though the effort hurt his chest. Apparently he'd have a steering-wheel-shaped bruise for the next couple of weeks.

A soft laugh came from the direction of Darcie's head and then stopped. "Ow. Laughing hurts. Help me get out of here, would you? There's something pushing on my back and I can't straighten up."

"That's the roof of the truck. It's amazing you weren't crushed. If you hadn't bent over…" The horror of what might have happened to them clogged his throat.

Thank You, Lord.

"Here, hold on."

The driver's door had been pushed inward, which

limited the available space in the cab. He slid sideways, the steering wheel rubbing against his raw chest. Shattered glass covered everything, so he grabbed the first thing he could find to brush it away, the soggy, bent cardboard top of Darcie's shoe box. Where the rest of the box was he didn't know. Rain poured over his head and down his face.

Shouts from outside reached him as he pressed the release button on her seat belt buckle. "I think somebody's coming to help."

"I hope they have an aspirin. Ouch. This stupid collar is stabbing the back of my neck."

"Here. Let me help."

With difficulty, Caleb helped her scoot gingerly sideways. When she was free of the mangled roof, he pressed himself against the crushed door to allow her room to straighten. Rain plastered her hair to her scalp, but she raised her face toward the sky.

"Oh, that feels…" She winced, and drew in her breath with a hiss. "Awful, actually. If I'd know I'd have to bend over in the shape of a hairpin, I would have taken up yoga or something to limber up."

Help arrived in the form of a pair of men who approached in a half run, half slide down the soggy embankment. Two anxious faces peered at them through the missing windshield.

"Everybody okay in there?" one of them asked.

"I think so," Caleb answered. "But we're going to need help getting out."

"Hang tight," said the other man. "We've called for an ambulance."

A third person approached. "How bad is it?" he shouted over the noise of the rain.

"Nobody's dead," answered the first man. "Hey, can I have that?"

The onslaught of rain ceased a minute later when a black umbrella appeared over the missing windshield.

"Thanks, brother." To Darcie he said, "Scoot over this way."

He slid sideways on the seat to give her as much room beneath the shelter as possible, then held an arm wide in an invitation to huddle close.

She didn't hesitate before settling into the crook of his arm. His stomach somersaulted when she relaxed against his chest and the back of her head pressed against his chin. Could she hear the thunder of his heart, or would she think it was rain thudding against the umbrella?

"I hear a siren," said one of their rescuers. "The ambulance is almost here."

Caleb listened. "That's not an ambulance." In a lower voice, he told Darcie, "That's a police siren."

"Great," she muttered. "I wonder how long before Detective Samuels shows up."

"Well, look at it like this. He might actually believe us now."

"I don't believe you two!" The detective planted both hands on the conference table and leaned across, bulging eyes fixed on Darcie. "I've told you over and over to stay out of this investigation, and what did you do? You ignored me. A blatant disrespect for my authority."

After an ambulance ride to the hospital emergency room and several hours of waiting for a doctor to examine them, Darcie and Caleb had been released. Caleb had suffered a bruised rib and had a dozen stitches in his left arm from broken glass. Darcie was sore, stiff and bruised, but otherwise unharmed. The doctor had pronounced her "extraordinarily lucky," to which Caleb had replied, "I don't believe in luck. I believe in God." After seeing the mangled truck roof and contemplating what would have happened had she not been bent forward, Darcie was inclined to agree with him.

The detective's glare switched to Caleb. "The first thing you did was pull strings to arrange an off-the-record visit to a *state prison.*"

"He is my uncle," Darcie offered tentatively, which drew the ambivalent stare back to her.

"Oh? So you're telling me that was nothing more than a family visitation? A devoted niece visiting her favorite uncle in prison?"

Darcie flushed.

"I thought not." The detective jerked a chair out from beneath the table and dropped into it, fury doing battle on his face.

Darcie couldn't stop glancing at the mirrored wall. Were there officers on the other side of that glass, watching the interrogation? Probably. They'd certainly attracted attention when the policeman who'd picked them up at the hospital delivered them to the police headquarters and Samuels.

"I ought to lock you both up." He stabbed a finger toward Caleb. "Especially you."

The big man's calm expression did not change. "I can understand you feeling that way."

Apparently the answer was not what the detective expected to hear. Quizzical lines creased his forehead, and his face lost some of the furious purple. He heaved a loud sigh. "All right. It appears someone besides me isn't happy with you two. Tell me what you've got."

Darcie read triumph in Caleb's eyes when they connected with hers for a second before he answered, "Not much, I'm afraid. A lot of questions, not many answers."

She listened as he recounted their steps since Samuels left the Emersons' yesterday morning. The detective's thumb stroked his chin while he listened. He interrupted only once, when Caleb mentioned the underground room, deliberately glossing over the details of how they'd discovered its existence.

"Who told you about this room?"

Caleb's gaze slid toward the mirrors. "I promised not to say."

Samuels's eyebrows inched upward, but he waved for Caleb to continue. He ended with a description of being forced over the embankment.

"I don't believe for one minute that the Fairmonts are involved in anything illegal." The detective's glare turned pensive. "But I admit there are some things that need to be looked into." He looked at Darcie. "You're sure you don't have anything else that Fairmont gave your mother? Just the dog?"

She hesitated only a moment before sliding the ring off of her finger. "Only this. Uncle Richard said it was worth around two hundred dollars. Those are real emerald chips, but they're awfully small."

After a close examination of the ring, he handed it back to her. "The stamp inside says it's only fourteen-karat gold. Can't imagine anyone trying to kill you over that."

Relieved, she slipped the ring back on her finger.

Another long moment of silence, and then Samuels blew out a breath through pursed lips. "Well, I don't see any way around it. I'm going to have to get a warrant to take a look at that underground room, but I don't look forward to explaining to the judge why I need to disturb Richard Fairmont's widow." He glanced at his wristwatch. "I'm not going to call him tonight, though. First thing in the morning's soon enough."

He put his hands on the table and pushed himself out of the chair. "If I were you two, I wouldn't go home. I doubt if whoever is responsible will attempt anything else tonight, but you never know. I can offer you the city's accommodations at the jail, but I doubt if you'd like the facilities or your roommates."

Spend a night in jail? Darcie shuddered. "Thanks anyway."

"I'll get a patrolman to take you wherever you want to go and tell them to keep an eye out for you tonight."

With that, the door behind him opened to reveal an officer standing in the doorway. She glanced at the mirror. As she suspected.

When Samuels swept out, Caleb rose gingerly from his chair, wincing, his left arm held protectively against his rib cage. "He's right. We need to find a place for the night. I'd rather not go back to Brent and Lauren's, just in case the goons have been watching us. I'll give Mason a call. Hopefully they won't know about his place."

He reached for his pocket, but then patted it. "My cell phone is still in the truck."

"My purse is, too, and the shoe box." Tears blurred her vision when she thought of Mama's treasures deserted in the rain-soaked, mangled vehicle. She turned tear-filled eyes on Caleb. "Can we go get them?"

His expression became gentle. "Of course we can. Let's find a phone."

"I hope you'll be comfortable," Karina told Darcie an hour later. "My brother's room isn't as fancy as Lauren's guest room, but the bed is soft."

Darcie examined the sports pennants on the wall. A model airplane lay halfway assembled, parts scattered across the surface of a desk in one corner next to a video game console.

She turned toward Karina. "I hope your brother doesn't mind being put out of his room."

Karina dismissed her concern. "He's spending the night with a friend down the street, so the timing's perfect."

Though Darcie wouldn't call anything about this disastrous week perfect, she nodded anyway.

Mason had come to the police station to get them and brought her here. He and Caleb had verified that the wrecked pickup hadn't been towed yet and then headed over to retrieve their belongings, leaving her in Karina's care.

"The bathroom's down the hall, and I put clean towels on the vanity." Her hostess studied Darcie's figure through narrowed eyes. "I'm bigger than you, but not too much. I'll get you something to wear for the night."

She turned to leave, but Darcie stopped her with a hand on her arm. "Thank you. You and Lauren have been so kind to me, and I want you to know I appreciate it."

"We're happy to help." A knowing glint appeared in the dark eyes fixed on her. "Especially for a friend of Caleb's."

A blush threatened at the openly prying gaze.

Darcie looked away. "Caleb has a lot of friends, doesn't he?"

"Yes, he does."

Disappointment stabbed at her.

Then Karina's smile deepened. "But not many female friends. You're the only one he's ever introduced to us."

"Really?"

She tried to make the word casual, nonchalant. Apparently she failed, because Karina giggled and squeezed her hand. "Really. He likes you. A lot."

She wasn't talking about friendship. Fear flared to life in a deep place in Darcie's heart. She shook her head. "You're wrong. He's only helping me because he happened to be in the wrong place at the wrong time."

The smile still hovering around Karina's lips proved she didn't agree. "I'll bet when this is all over—"

Darcie interrupted, not rudely but firmly, "I'm leaving Atlanta as soon as I can. Caleb knows that."

She avoided Karina's eyes but was aware that the amused smile remained. "If you say so. Why don't you go ahead and take a shower? I'll be right back with those clothes. When you're out, we can have a cup of herbal tea and talk."

"Thanks."

A hot shower was exactly what Darcie needed to soothe her bruised and battered body. She left her watch and ring on the nightstand and spent fifteen minutes standing under the spray, willing the hot water to wash the tension out of her aching muscles.

Finally, cleaner and warmer and dressed in Karina's soft T-shirt and stretchy pants, Darcie wandered around the bedroom, examining the evidence of a teenage boy's presence in the room. But her mind hovered around a mature man. Over the past few days Caleb had done more than befriend her. Somehow in the midst of all the trauma, he had pierced through the shield she'd erected around her heart. She hadn't even been looking for someone to prove to her that a man could be trustworthy and kind, but that's exactly what she'd found. Her emotions were still raw from the death of the one person who had ever loved her unconditionally. But for the first time since Mama had died, she felt a faint hope that eventually the pain would heal, that one day she'd be ready to open her heart and let someone else in.

Was that someone Caleb?

She idly straightened a stack of CDs on the top of a small stereo. And yet, there was something between them, some obstacle she couldn't identify. As strong as Caleb was, she sensed a vulnerability in him that held him back. Maybe one day, when this ordeal was behind them, they could—

A creak behind her. For an instant, her heart froze. Someone was in the room. She sprinted for the door, her mouth opened to scream.

The sound never came. A hand clamped over her

mouth. The terror from the restaurant parking lot returned with blinding force. Only this time, Caleb wasn't there to help her.

EIGHTEEN

The rain had stopped by the time Caleb and Mason arrived at the crash site. Armed with flashlights against the darkness, they slipped their way down soggy grass to the mangled pickup.

Mason shined a beam over the crumpled cab and gave a low whistle. "That is one messed up hunk of metal. I hope you've got good insurance."

"I hope so, too." Shattered glass covering the seat reflected Caleb's light when he shone it through the driver's window. "I don't see my phone. Here, hold this a minute."

He handed the flashlight to Mason and grabbed the handle. The door moved but didn't open. "It's stuck fast."

"Got a tire iron?"

"Yeah."

The keys were still in the ignition. Leaning carefully over broken shards of glass in the window, and wincing at the pain in his ribs, Caleb grabbed them. The padlock on the toolbox in the truck bed was undamaged. He dug through tools and found the tire iron. The sound of bending metal creaked into the night as he pried open the door.

"No sign of my phone," he told Mason, shining his light around the cramped interior. "It probably flew out when we flipped. There's Darcie's purse, though."

When he bent over to retrieve the purse, jewels winked in his flashlight beam. He picked up the tacky dog collar. The shoe box was nothing more than a soggy mass of cardboard, but at least the contents were still inside. He scooped it up and exited the cab.

They got the toolbox unhooked from the truck bed and carried it up the hill to Mason's car and then left. As Mason navigated the freeway, Caleb fingered the green stones on the collar.

"Wouldn't it be funny if these were real emeralds and diamonds?"

Mason laughed. "Wouldn't that be a kick? Fairmont smuggling jewels along with the froufrou dogs his wife sells."

Caleb stared at him as the words settled in his mind. He flipped on the flashlight and shone it on the collar. Certainly those were not real diamonds. They didn't sparkle the way real ones did. What about the emeralds, though? He sure had seen a lot of them lately. Those emerald chips in Darcie's ring. The huge ones dangling from Olivia Fairmont's ears and neck.

Mason noticed his concentration, "I know what

you're thinking, but those are definitely not emeralds. If you have a hammer in your toolbox you can prove it. Emeralds aren't as hard as diamonds, but they're pretty hard."

Excitement mounting, Caleb turned around and dug in his toolbox for his hammer. Darcie would probably be furious, but he had to know. He braced the collar against the dashboard, took aim with his hammer and—

Crunch. The green stone crushed on impact.

"Told you so." Mason wore a smug expression. "They're green-colored glass."

"Okay, okay. I was wrong."

But when he'd put the hammer away, he couldn't rid his mind of the idea that emeralds were an important clue. He shone the flashlight into every green stone on the collar, but none of them looked any different from the one he'd smashed. Still...

"Can I use your phone, brother?"

"Sure."

Mason handed it over, and Caleb dialed a number. Brent answered on the second ring. He sounded relieved to hear Caleb's voice and wanted to know how bad the damage to the truck was.

"It's trashed," Caleb told him. "I called to ask you to look something up for me on the internet. Find out anything you can about emerald smuggling."

"Sure." Brent sounded curious. "I've shut down already, so give me a minute to boot up. I'll call you back."

Caleb disconnected the call but held on to the phone.

Mason shook his head. "If you ask me, you're barking up the wrong tree, dude."

"Probably. But right now it's the only tree I can see."

They'd almost reached the house when Brent called back.

"What'd you find?" In spite of himself, Caleb held his breath.

"Not much," Brent said. "The feds apparently don't focus much on gem smuggling unless it's connected somehow to drugs or money laundering or organized crime. They estimate the market value of illegal gems in the U.S. at somewhere around 788 million dollars, which is small potatoes."

Caleb let out the breath. "Ah, well. Thanks for looking."

Brent warmed to his topic. "I did find an interesting fact, though. The Colombian government says the value of illegal emerald exports from their country was close to two billion dollars a decade ago. About six years ago they cracked down on the smugglers, so they're losing less now."

Interesting maybe, but helpful? Not so much.

"It was worth a try. Thanks, buddy."

He hung up, thoughts whirling. Six years ago. That would be about a year before Kenneth Pryor was arrested for embezzlement. About a year before the construction of the Fairmont's kennel and underground room.

He shook his head, trying to make his thoughts fall into some sort of order. Something was missing, but what?

Mason pulled the car into his garage. Caleb gathered the things he'd rescued from the truck and followed him into the house, where Karina waited.

"Sit there." She pointed to one of the stools around the kitchen island and placed a mug in front of him. The string of an herbal tea bag hung over the side. When she poured steaming water over it, Caleb drew the relaxing scent of mint chamomile into his lungs.

But there was no relaxing tonight.

"Where's Darcie?" he asked.

"I think she went to bed." Karina's brow wrinkled. "I thought she was going to get dressed and come out for a cup of tea after her shower, but I guess she changed her mind."

"She's probably exhausted, poor kid." Mason opened the refrigerator and inspected the contents. "We got anything to eat?"

"Have a mug of tea," Karina told him. "It'll fill you up."

"Okay." He emerged from the fridge with a package of ham and a brick of cheese. "It'll wash down my sandwich."

Caleb smiled absently at Karina's expansive eye roll, but his thoughts were elsewhere. What if Pryor's "insurance" was proof that the Fairmonts were gem smugglers?

"What's this?" Karina picked up the collar.

"Oh, it's some sort of fancy status symbol that came with Darcie's dog."

"Huh." She held it up to the light to inspect it closer. "Well, I wouldn't put it on my dog, but then again, I wouldn't pay a thousand dollars for a puppy, either." With a finger, she tapped the jewel-encrusted barrel. "That's cute. What do they put in the real dog barrels, anyway?"

"Brandy," answered Mason as he sliced off a thick chunk of cheese. "Saint Bernards were trained to find people lost in avalanches. The brandy was supposed to keep them warm until help arrived."

Caleb watched the dangling barrel swing. If he were trapped in a snowstorm, he'd rather have hot chocolate or coffee or—

He went still. They put brandy *inside* the dog's barrel.

"You don't suppose…" He held his hand out for the collar. "Let me see that for a minute."

Alerted by the intensity in his voice, Mason stopped slicing to watch as Caleb examined the barrel charm. It wasn't big, about two inches long and maybe an inch and a half wide. Tiny gem chips covered the sides, but he didn't spare more than a cursory glance at those. Of course they weren't real. Nobody would be stupid enough to glue real emeralds on the outside of a dog collar. But inside…

"Mason, do you have a small flat-head screwdriver?"

Mason abandoned his sandwich and dashed out

of the room. He returned with a tool kit, the kind used for eyeglasses. Caleb selected the smallest screwdriver and inserted the tip into a tiny indentation he found in the edge of the barrel. With a twist of the handle, one end of the barrel popped off like the back of a wristwatch.

Shoved inside the barrel was a piece of gray felt. He grabbed a corner between his fingers and pulled it out. Not merely a piece, but a small drawstring bag. And inside…

Karina gasped aloud when he emptied a mound of gleaming green stones into the palm of his hand. No mistaking these for glass. Their faceted surfaces caught the overhead light and tossed green fire into the air.

"You'd better go wake Darcie." His voice was hoarse, husky.

Karina hurried out of the room.

"Dude, look at the size of that one." Mason bent close to inspect the stones. "It's got to be five carats. And the others are at least a carat or two each."

"How much do you suppose these are worth?" Caleb asked.

"Hard to tell. It depends on the clarity and color and all kinds of things, but I'd guess at least two grand per carat."

Which meant Caleb was holding a small fortune in the palm of his hand.

"Caleb! Mason!" Karina's shout preceded her into

the room. When she appeared, her eyes were wide. "Darcie's gone."

"What?"

Caleb jumped off the stool and ran down the short hallway. The door stood open, and the bedroom was empty.

"She told me she was going to leave Atlanta." Karina's voice held tears. "But I thought she meant later, after the case was solved."

His heart plummeted. Whirling, he sought Karina's face. "She said she was leaving?"

A hand over her mouth, she nodded. "But I'm sure she meant when this was over. I'm sure of it."

He turned toward the wall to wage a private battle with his thoughts. He'd been right about her all along. The first day he'd met her he knew she was a runner. Just like Anita. The way they dealt with a problem was to run away from it.

And just like Anita, she'd taken a piece of his heart with her when she ran.

Why, Lord? Why did You let this happen? I trusted You not to let this happen to me again.

He'd been betrayed, just like the last time. Not once but twice. By Darcie and by God. It was almost enough to bring him to his knees. His fist tightened, and the stones in his hand cut into his palm.

Then he spied something on the nightstand.

Leaping forward, he snatched the ring. Tiny green stones sparkled in the dim light of the lamp, miniature versions of the ones he'd removed from the collar.

Whirling, he held the ring aloft. "She didn't leave on her own. She would never leave her mother's ring behind."

The impact of his statement struck him hard. His arm fell to his side. "She's been kidnapped."

NINETEEN

Darcie sat on the floor of the van, her hands and mouth bound with duct tape. The cloth the man had stuffed into her mouth back in the bedroom stank and tasted of sweat. Her stomach threatened to heave, but she fought against the nausea. If she vomited she'd probably choke, and the man in the ski mask sitting across from her would no doubt enjoy watching her die. It would save him the trouble of killing her.

She closed her eyes but could still feel the weight of those cold eyes staring at her.

"How close are we?" Her captor's voice raked like gravel across her fear-sensitive ears.

The answer came from the driver's seat. "Ten minutes."

"You better call."

"I'm driving. You call."

The man in the back with her gave a disgusted grunt, but she heard the tones of cell phone keys being punched and then the faint sound of a phone ringing through a tiny speaker.

"Got her." The kidnapper who'd dragged her through the bedroom window at Karina's house clipped the words short but in a more subdued tone than he'd used when speaking to the driver. "We're ten minutes out."

A muffled voice answered, but she couldn't make out the reply.

"Understood." A shuffle and then he said to the driver, "Go the back way."

"What do you think I am, an idiot? Of course I'm going in the back. You think I want to mess around with Caesar? That dog's nuts when he's on guard duty."

When she heard that, Darcie knew where they were taking her. Caesar must be the rottweiler who guarded Fairmont Estate at night. Of course. Where else would they take her but to the secret room beneath the pool house? And who would she meet there? Mrs. Fairmont? Dread mounted inside her.

"We have to go right now." Caleb's fist slammed down on the kitchen counter so hard Karina jumped.

Detective Samuels wasn't intimidated. He shoved a finger in Caleb's face. "You calm down, you hear me? We'll handle this my way."

"But you're not doing anything." Frustration boiled in his stomach, but Caleb forced himself to lower his voice. "They've taken her to that underground room."

"You don't know that."

He ran a hand roughly across his scalp. "Where else would they go? They're going to take her someplace where we can't find her, and they think nobody knows about that room."

"Who is this *they* you keep talking about? If you have a name, give it to me. Give me someplace to start."

Caleb threw a hand in the air. "I don't know! Start with Mrs. Fairmont. She's the one selling dogs with jewels stuffed in their collars. Go get her out of bed and ask her to explain that. And while you're there, find that underground room."

His voice rose to a shouting pitch, and Karlna stepped forward to place a warning hand on his arm. Caleb fought against the rising urgency that vibrated in every muscle of his body.

When he had regained control, Samuels nodded. "That's better. Now, listen to me a minute. We can't wake Mrs. Fairmont up to question her because she's not home. When her husband died, she told me she was going to stay with her sister in Stone Mountain for a few days."

"Good," Caleb shot back. "Then nobody's there to see if you search the pool house. Let's go."

Samuels rolled his eyes and said to Mason, who stood nearby, "You used to be a cop, didn't you? Talk sense to him."

Mason caught and held Caleb's eye. "Dude, you know they can't search without a warrant. If they find anything it'll get thrown out of court."

Caleb gritted his teeth and said to the detective, "Then wake up the judge and get a warrant."

"I'm heading there right now," Samuels said. "But not until I'm sure you're going to stay out of trouble and out of my way. You are not to leave this house, do you understand me, Buchanan?"

His eyes held Caleb's in a steely trap. Without a doubt, he wouldn't leave without a promise that Caleb wouldn't strike out on his own the minute he was gone. But Caleb couldn't promise that.

Do I understand you?

Yeah, he understood the detective's order. He had no intention of obeying, but he understood. He nodded.

That satisfied Samuels. "Good. I'll call when I know something."

He left the kitchen, and Caleb stayed where he was, tracking his progress by sound. He heard the front door open, and then Samuels's voice speaking to someone outside before the door closed.

The home phone rang. Karina answered and then put her hand over the mouthpiece. "It's Brent. He wants an update."

Caleb shook his head. He couldn't talk right now, not even to his friends. He knew what they'd say, that he should wait here and let Samuels do his job. Given different circumstances he'd agree with them. But this was Darcie's life he was talking about. He'd promised to keep her safe. Was he going to sit around and twiddle his thumbs all night? Not a chance.

Taking the receiver from Karina, Mason looked at him and spoke into the phone. "Yeah, he's doing okay. I mean, as good as you or I would do in the same situation." Brent said something, and Mason sauntered casually from the room. Caleb heard him speaking in a low voice as he headed toward the bedroom. With a quick smile in his direction, Karina followed.

The minute she was out of sight, Caleb acted. Mason's car keys and cell phone sat on the counter where he'd laid them when they had returned home from the crash site. Caleb snatched them up, pocketed the phone and then whirled to jerk the refrigerator open. Thoughts fired through the inside of his brain like bullets. He'd need to create some sort of distraction for when he got to the Fairmont Estate. There. Next to the ham was a package of hot dogs.

He could no longer hear Mason's voice from the other room. Had he hung up the phone? Caleb didn't stick around to find out. With three long strides he passed through the family room on his way to the garage and snatched up one of the big throw pillows from the sofa. A plan was forming. Not a good plan, and not one he was looking forward to. But at least he would be doing something to help Darcie.

From her position on the floor, Darcie couldn't see outside the van but she felt the moment they left the main road and pulled onto another paved surface. When the driver turned off the lights, she assumed they were entering the Fairmont Estate by a rear entrance, since they'd been instructed to come in the back way. Why were they entering under the cover of darkness, though? They were expected, weren't they?

In a few minutes the van slowed, and she heard a dog barking, a deep, ferocious sound. Caesar? Then even the little bit of light in the van went dark as the vehicle pulled into an enclosure of some sort.

"I'm not setting a foot out there until he gets that animal under control," said the driver.

"There he is."

The dog's barking stopped, and the man in the back of the van with her slid open the door. The dome light illuminated, and Darcie blinked to adjust her eyes. Her captor pulled off his ski mask. Though she wasn't surprised, she couldn't stop a gasp when she caught sight of his face. The stranger who'd watched her house in Indiana and who'd followed her to Atlanta.

His lips curled into an unpleasant grin. "Recognize me, do you?"

She wasn't given time to answer before he slipped a hand beneath one arm and hauled her forward. She was dragged out of the van, and the dog began barking again, this time with a frantic edge.

"You got a good hold of him?" The van's driver leaned out of the open door.

A male voice came from the shadows nearby. Not Mrs. Fairmont then. "Caesar, attack."

The dog's barking took on a frenzied tone, punctuated by snarls.

"Hey, that ain't funny," said the driver, raw fear apparent in his voice.

His answer was a laugh. "Just bring her. I won't let the big, mean dog get you. Caesar, stay." The last was uttered in a commanding tone.

She found herself being propelled forward. When she exited the building she immediately recognized her surroundings. The structure beside her housed the Fairmont Kennel. They'd just exited the barn-shaped garage at the opposite end from the pool house.

A dozen or so fluffy white puppies ran through doggie doors into their fenced yards, yapping an excited greeting.

"Shhhh, quiet, you mutts." Her captor shoved her forward. "You'll wake the missus."

"Don't worry about that. Just get her down to the lab."

Fear dropped into her belly as she was propelled forward, past the row of dog kennels toward the pool house. The underground room housed a lab?

TWENTY

Mason's cell phone rang. Caleb knew the identity of the caller without looking. With one hand on the wheel, he punched the button to answer.

"I know what you're going to say." He executed a curve, watching the speedometer. Not too fast or he'd attract attention, even though every fiber in his body urged speed.

"Dude, you stole my car!" Outrage gave Mason's voice volume.

"Remember the time you borrowed my truck to pick up your new washer and drier?"

A pause. "Yeah, so?"

"So I'm calling in the favor. I'll return your car when I have Darcie back."

"You are one crazy guy, you know that? That cop is going to go ballistic when he finds out you're going to the Fairmonts'."

"By the time he gets the paperwork together and wakes the judge for a warrant, I'll have Darcie and we'll be back at your house."

"Caleb." The voice on the other side of the phone was Mason at his most serious. "What if she's not there?"

"I know she is."

"How? How do you know that?"

He could describe the feeling of absolute certainty that had settled deep in his gut. Mason would understand that. He was a brother, a fellow believer in the power of God. But the truth was, Caleb wasn't at all sure this feeling was God. Maybe it was nothing but him, his own desire to keep his promise to Darcie. Since the day he had met her, his feelings had turned upside down. But one thing he was sure of. He couldn't sit around and do nothing while she was in danger.

"If I'm wrong," he told Mason, "then I'm no worse off than now. I'll find an empty building and I'll come home."

"You're wrong about that, buddy. In about an hour the cops are going to swarm all over that place and you'll end up in jail for trespassing and obstruction and whatever else that detective wants to throw at you."

For that, he had no answer. If he was wrong, if the men who'd abducted Darcie had taken her someplace else…he couldn't bear to think about the consequences.

Mason's voice took on a tone of resignation. "All right. I get it. I'd probably act like an idiot, too, if I were in your shoes. Pull over the next place you can and wait for me. I'll call Brent and we'll be there as soon as we can. Friends don't let friends act stupid alone."

Caleb smiled at the offer. Mason and Brent were good friends, the best a guy could have. And there was no doubt in his mind that he could use their help. But he couldn't drag them into a situation like this, not when both of them had wives who cared for them.

"Thanks, brother, but by the time you get there, it'll be all over. Stay home. I'll call you when I have her."

He ended the call and tossed the phone in the passenger seat. It rang again immediately, but he ignored it.

Once he left the more populated area of the city, Caleb pushed the car as much as he dared. A half mile from the Fairmont Estate he pulled off the road and parked beneath a tree. From his toolbox, which was still in Mason's backseat, he took a short coil of rope he kept stashed there and shoved it into a canvas nail pouch. An umbrella lay on the floorboard, and he added that as well as the wieners. So armed, he grabbed the pillow and abandoned the car to run the rest of the way, one hand pressed against his injured rib for support. With every step that took him closer, his fear mounted. He was about to do the one thing he dreaded most in the world.

"Lord, You and I both know what's on the other side of that fence around the Fairmont place." His words bounced out as he ran, wincing against the pain the activity caused. "Now, I don't know if You've gone quiet on me lately, or if I just haven't been listening like I should. But I can't do this alone. I need You."

As the last words left his mouth, he approached the corner of Fairmont Estate. A white plank fence marked the border here and all the way around, as far as he could see. A thick stand of trees blocked his sight of the mansion, which he knew lay at the end of the long, curving driveway.

A sound in the distance drew his attention. A barking dog. His ears strained to pinpoint the location. A chill marched up his spine when he realized the barking was growing louder. A moving shadow, illuminated by white moonlight, was heading toward him at an alarming speed, snarling between barks.

"I need You, Lord." He repeated the words in a louder voice, then for good measure, tilted his head back and directed them toward the sky. "I need You."

The dog arrived at the fence. For a moment Caleb thought it might leap over the top to get to him, but it skidded to a halt and fixed its eyes on him, snarling and barking its fury. Apparently it had been trained to stay inside the fence.

Unfortunately, that's where Caleb needed to be.

The snarls reached through his ears and tugged at a memory. He was nine, and the dog down the street had sounded just like this one. Fear reached inside Caleb's rib cage and squeezed his heart with steely fingers.

Fear not. That's what the Bible says.

Yeah, but he couldn't think of a single Scripture reference to attacking dogs. Lions, yes. Bears, certainly. Before his giant-killing days, David the shepherd boy fought off a bear to save his sheep.

"Uh, Lord, if You have a bear handy, I think I'd rather fight that."

Some corner of his brain recognized that he desperately wanted to laugh, but he squashed the impulse. Laughter was too close to hysteria.

"All right, look here, dog. I don't have time to mess around. I've got somewhere to be, and you're in my way."

The animal's barking trailed off into a rumbling growl. Its eyes glowed in the moonlight. Moving slowly, Caleb reached into the nail pouch and fumbled with the package of hot dogs.

"Look here, doggie. Look what I have for you. Are you hungry?"

He held a wiener up, waving it back and forth to get the creature's attention. "Here you are. It's all yours. Go get it."

With a toss, he flicked the hot dog over the fence to a spot eight feet away.

The dog never even blinked, nor was there a pause in the menacing growl. So much for bribery. With a sinking feeling in the pit of his stomach, Caleb realized there was only one way to get past this animal.

Looping the rope around his arm, he closed his eyes.

All kidding aside, Lord, You know I'm scared spitless of this animal.

He felt it then, the touch he hadn't felt for days. An assurance, deep and warm, resonated in his soul. His fear didn't dissipate, but suddenly he realized that it didn't matter. David probably faced that bear with his knees knocking and his hands trembling, but he had been confident that his God wouldn't desert him.

Nor would He desert Caleb.

Holding the pillow like a shield and Mason's umbrella like a sword, he advanced toward the fence.

Darcie's breath came heavy through her nose. She tried in vain to spit the nasty rag out of her mouth, but the duct tape held fast to her skin. She was led roughly past the excited puppies and pulled through the kennel manager's office door. Her gaze flew to the spot where she had seen Jason Lewis's body. Which of these three men had killed him, and Uncle Richard, too? With a dreadful certainty, she knew she was about to find out.

Her captor shoved her through another doorway, and she found herself inside the pool house. She barely had time to notice a wicker patio set facing a wall of curtains that hid the pool from view. The driver of the van opened a door and stepped into a closet. Interested in spite of herself, she watched him feel along the floor and then lift a carpeted, hinged panel. He disappeared into a yawning black hole, and a moment later a white light flickered on. She glimpsed a narrow set of steep stairs.

"Ms. Wiley, you're about to discover something interesting about your rich uncle."

That voice. Where did she know it? It came to her an instant before Aaron Mitchell stepped into view.

Of course. How stupid not to have guessed. Who else would know the conditions of Uncle Richard's will but his financial manager? And if he was trusted with the details of the will, no doubt he'd also been told the reason behind the special bequest to a young woman from Indiana.

"Bring her down."

Mitchell descended the stairs, and Darcie was pushed forward after him. Her captor wrapped a fist in the T-shirt at the back of her neck.

"I'll carry you if I have to." His lips were so close to her ear she felt the warmth of his breath on her cheek. With a shudder, she descended the stairway.

The room below was stark, bare of all furniture except four folding chairs and a card table. A wide counter lined two of the walls, the surface crowded with pieces of equipment that Darcie had never seen before. A half-dozen huge steel canisters with gauges and dials affixed to the sides and thin pipes spiraling out of the tops put her in mind of pictures of illegal stills in the Appalachian mountains. Only these had a sterile, modern look. A low, electric hum emanated from them.

"So here you have it." Mitchell stood in the center, his hands splayed to indicate the room. "Our little laboratory."

A morbid curiosity settled atop the fear that had congealed in her belly. What was the function of those machines? Was this some sort of human experimentation laboratory like the Nazis operated during the war? Two men were dead, and more than likely she would follow soon. Was that why they'd brought her here, to do some sort of horrible experiment on her before they killed her?

Lord, I don't know if You're there or not, but Caleb says You are. Please don't let them torture me. If I have to die, let it be quick.

Mitchell was watching her closely. "I see you have questions. If we take the gag off, do you promise not to scream?"

She could say yes, and then when they removed the nasty rag from her mouth, she'd scream like a banshee.

"It won't do you any good if you do," Mitchell told her. "No one will hear you. This room is as good as soundproof. A gun could go off down here and it wouldn't even sound as loud as a firecracker outside the pool house. In fact." He opened a metal drawer in the nearest cabinet and took out a pistol. Waving it in her direction, he asked, "Would you like a demonstration?"

Her shoulders sagged. It didn't occur to her to doubt him. Being underground no doubt acted as a muffler to sound, and the room had the heavy, dull feel of soundproofing. Defeated, she shook her head.

Mitchell nodded toward her captor. "Butch, take the gag off but leave her hands taped."

"Hey, don't use my name in front of her," he protested.

"It doesn't matter, imbecile. She's not going to tell anyone."

His meaning was clear, even without the gun waving in her direction. Very shortly, she wouldn't be alive to tell anyone anything. The tears that flooded her eyes were only partially due to the pain when Butch ripped the tape off, taking hair and pieces of tender skin around her lips with it.

"There. I'm sure that's better. Now, I know you have questions."

But Darcie didn't trust herself to speak without giving way to the terrified sobs that threatened to choke her.

"Oh, come on. You know you want to ask about these." He waved the gun toward the odd-looking canisters. "Okay, I'll tell you. These are crucibles. The cores are platinum, though they could have been constructed of any nonreactive material that can withstand high temperatures and pressure. But Richard wanted nothing but the best, so…" He shrugged. "Platinum."

In spite of her determination to remain silent, she asked a question. "Uncle Richard set up this lab?"

"Well, he didn't do it himself, of course. He paid to have it built and paid for the equipment. Had these designed and shipped up from China, I understand, though that was before my time." He aimed a chilly smile her way. "If you want to know about that, your uncle can give you the details."

She knew without asking which uncle he referred to. "Uncle Kenneth."

"My illustrious predecessor." Mitchell's lip curled. "Not the sharpest knife in the drawer, but he had guts, I'll give him that. Why Richard let him take the rap for embezzlement instead of having him killed, I'll never know."

"Take the rap? You mean he didn't steal Uncle Richard's money?"

"Of course he did. But he did far worse than that. When he was caught, he threatened to expose Richard to the Colombians."

Darcie shook her head. "I don't know what you mean. Expose him for what?"

Behind her, Butch growled, "Can we get on with this? It's getting late. What if they've figured out she's gone by now? The cops will be swarming everywhere."

"Relax. They won't find us down here." Regardless of his words, Mitchell's attitude changed. He dropped the conversational tone and spoke to Darcie in a voice void of patience. "Where's the collar?"

Her mind struggled to make sense of the question. He could only mean Percy's collar, but what did that have to do with Uncle Richard and this secret laboratory?

"I—I don't have it," she stammered. "It was in the truck when we crashed."

He looked at the third man, the one who had driven the van and was now seated at the card table. "Go get it."

The man jerked upright. "Me? No way."

Mitchell's eyes narrowed. "Who was the brain who decided to run them off the road?"

"Hey, it was storming. I saw a chance and I took it. But then those other cars stopped, and what was I supposed to do? Hang around and get nailed?"

The gun swung toward him. "Go get the collar. Now."

Fear flickered in the man's eyes. Without another word he got up and headed for the stairs.

When he had gone, Darcie gathered her nerve to ask a question. If she was going to die, then she at least wanted to understand why.

"What are these machines?"

A genuine smile curved his lips. "Here. Let me show you."

The gun still in one hand, he walked to a corner of the room. Darcie had been so intent on watching him she had not noticed a small safe tucked beneath the wide countertop. Samuels stooped in front of it and twisted the dial. Left, right, left. He grabbed the lever, turned it and pulled the door open. From inside he slid out a tray that looked like a cookie sheet.

Darcie's eyes widened. Those weren't cookies on that tray. They were emeralds.

TWENTY-ONE

Caleb backed away from the dog and examined his handiwork. The rottweiler continued to snarl, though the makeshift muzzle he'd fashioned out of rope didn't allow for its mouth to open wide enough for a full-throated bark. The end of the rope had been double-knotted around a fence post, which gave the animal about twelve feet of slack, but it strained toward him, stretching the tether to its limit. Every so often the snarl changed to a sound that could almost be interpreted as a pleading whine.

An unexpected sympathy chased away the last remnants of Caleb's fear. He squatted down on his haunches just beyond the dog's reach. "I'm sorry, fella, but those teeth of yours are lethal."

Proof lay scattered around the grass in the form of pillow stuffing and the mutilated remains of Mason's umbrella. They had served their purpose in distracting the dog long enough for Caleb to get hold of its nose and force its jaw closed, but he hadn't escaped unscathed. Blood dripped from a bite on his arm, almost exactly over the scar from that first dog attack sixteen years before.

He winced. It hurt like crazy, but in a weird way, he felt free. The fear that had gripped his insides was gone, leaving a strange sense of victory in his place. He'd prayed, and the Lord had heard him. Together they had conquered his bear.

"You'll be all right, fella. The only thing hurting you is your pride. I won't leave you here any longer than I have to. As soon as I can, I'll come back and let you go."

He extended a hand as a tentative peace offering. The dog lunged with such force that he feared the rope might snap, and Caleb fell backward, landing with a thud on his rear.

"Okay, okay. I'll send someone else to let you loose."

He scrambled to his feet. The encounter had taken no more than three or four minutes, but the panicky feeling vibrating through his body told him even that might have been too long. Darcie was in danger. He sprinted toward the house.

When he neared, he slowed and looped around in a wide arc. The outbuilding he'd painted a few days ago served as a good shelter and gave him a vantage point of this end of the pool house. He saw the faucet where he'd been cleaning his brushes when he'd first met Darcie. A quick scan of the area showed nothing else. No sound, either. A light shone dimly in one of the upstairs windows of the mansion. Probably on a timer or something, since the detective had said Mrs. Fairmont was staying with her sister. Whispering a quick prayer, he dashed across the grass and closed the distance as quickly as he could.

He flattened his back against the brick wall and crept to the corner, where he dropped to a crouch. He inched forward until he could see the back of the pool house building through one eye.

No movement. Nothing.

She has to be here! Lord, if she's not here...

He couldn't finish the thought.

The door to Lewis's office lay on the far side of the building, beneath the breezeway that connected it to the kennel. Between his position and that door there was no cover at all, not even a bush. No way to see what was on the other side of the building, either.

He'd have to take a chance.

Breath gathered in his lungs, he left the shelter of the building and dashed toward the door.

He'd almost made it when a dozen yapping dog voices shattered the silence. Little balls of fur tumbled out through a small rectangular doorway in the kennel and raced across the grass to the fence. They bounced and jumped on legs that must have been made of rubber, all the while barking with abandon.

"Shhh! Be quiet."

They ignored him. Alarm ringing in his ears nearly as loud as the pups, Caleb hurried to the door. He put his hand on the knob and turned. Unlocked.

Thank You, Lord.

A menacing metallic click behind him froze the blood in his veins. He knew that sound. It was the sound of a gun's hammer being cocked.

"Put your hands up and turn around. Slowly."

Caleb raised his hands above his head and, moving at a snail's pace, turned. The first thing he saw was a gun barrel pointed at his forehead. The second was the face of the gunman.

Correction. Gunwoman.

Olivia Fairmont.

Interested in spite of herself, Darcie studied the tray of gems Mitchell set on the counter. Some of those emeralds were huge like the ones Mrs. Fairmont had worn the other day, but most were a more realistic size for jewelry.

"I don't understand," she said. "You're smuggling emeralds? Then what are these gadgets for, polishing them?"

"Not even close." Mitchell's expression was smug. "We're not smuggling emeralds. We're making them."

Darcie looked again at the sparkling gems. "Those are fake?"

The smug grin faded. "Oh, no. They're quite real. Impossible to distinguish from the ones that come from Colombian mines. The process to create them is the same, only sped up by a few thousand years. These crucibles use a hydrothermal method of a water solution at high temperatures and pressure to create a batch of high-quality gems in a matter of months. It's perfectly legitimate. There are several well-respected companies that specialize in producing synthetic gems."

"Then why the secrecy?" She shook her head. "I don't understand."

"Because mineral gems sell at much higher prices than synthetic ones. Richard wasn't willing to settle for less."

"Uncle Richard knew about this?" She didn't want to believe it, but there was no hesitation in Mitchell's face when he replied.

"Of course he did. Didn't you hear me? He had the equipment manufactured and this lab built."

"But why?" She glanced toward the ceiling, above which stood the elaborate Fairmont Estate. "He didn't need the money."

"Money had nothing to do with it. It was the risk he thrived on. When he first got into the emerald business, the stones he sold were authentic, mined from Colombia and smuggled into this country."

"Uncle Richard was a gem smuggler?" Darcie couldn't believe the kind man she'd met would be involved in something illegal. His brother, yes. That wasn't hard to believe at all.

He did say he admired Ryan's daring ways and how he did whatever he wanted regardless of the consequences. Maybe there was a bit of that same daring in Uncle Richard, too.

"Both your uncles were gem smugglers. It was

Pryor who came up with the idea of distributing the gems inside the collars of those high-priced mutts Olivia breeds."

Inside the collars. Of course. She and Caleb had looked outside but not inside. She thought of sweet Mrs. Gates. "Do you mean everybody who buys a Fairmont Designer Dog is really buying emeralds?"

"Not every one. Just a few of them. Unfortunately, somebody made a stupid mistake." Mitchell glared at the man who had kidnapped her, who dropped his gaze for an intent inspection of the floor. "The collar sent to your mother had emeralds in it. We tried to switch it."

"Not my fault they never left that stupid house," mumbled the man.

Of course they didn't. Mama was dying of cancer and had decided to avoid hospitals so she could remain in her home until the end.

Darcie still didn't understand. "But why would he make emeralds if he had access to natural ones? Was he trying to become a legitimate manufacturer?"

That drew a laugh. "Legitimate? No. He switched because he was afraid. A few years ago his Colombian contacts got a little too difficult to deal with. Gems were only a sideline for them. Drugs are where the big money comes from, and they started applying pressure to convince Richard to expand from emeralds to cocaine. He wanted no part of that, but neither did he want to give up his emerald business. So he decided to create synthetic gems and pass them off as real ones."

It began to make sense. Darcie didn't want to believe Uncle Richard capable of illegal activities, but what did she really know about him? She had no difficulty picturing Uncle Kenneth threatening to betray him to drug-dealing Colombians. But instead of having him killed, Uncle Richard let him go to prison.

Well, at least he isn't a murderer. Or is he?

"Who killed Jason Lewis?" she asked.

"Him?" Mitchell shook his head. "He was an idiot. He discovered the lab and tried to blackmail Richard."

Horror bloomed in her chest. "You mean Uncle Richard killed him?"

Mitchell laughed. "No." The laughter died away, and the eyes fixed on Darcie became intense while his grip on the gun tightened. "I did."

"You." Recognition flared in Mrs. Fairmont's eyes when Caleb turned. "I knew there was something strange about you. Why did you kill Jason?"

Caleb kept his hands above his head, fingers splayed. "I didn't kill anyone. Honest."

"Huh." Clearly she didn't believe him. "What are you doing on my property?"

He would have liked to ask the same thing, since she'd told the detective she was staying with her sister for a few days, but obviously that had been a lie.

Instead he decided to confront her with something that mattered—the truth.

"I'm here to rescue Darcie. Where is she?"

Her head tilted slightly, confusion apparent in her eyes. "Darcie Wiley? What do you mean you're here to rescue her? Why would she be here?"

The response gave Caleb pause. Was this a ploy, a delay tactic? No, the woman looked genuinely confused.

"Not by choice—she's been kidnapped."

"Kidnapped?" No doubt her reaction to that news was genuine. Concern drew lines on her forehead, and the gun wavered uncertainly. "You need to contact the police immediately."

Caleb studied her. Was it possible she didn't know, that she wasn't involved? "I did contact the police. They're in the process of getting a search warrant from the judge, but I was afraid if I waited, it might be too late."

"Search warrant? For my kennel?"

"No," he said carefully, watching her reaction closely. "For the secret room beneath your pool house."

No mistaking that reaction. Her jaw dropped open and she lowered her hand to her side, the gun apparently forgotten. "What are you talking about?"

The puppies continued to raise a ruckus, desperately trying to get their attention. "Uh, can you shut them up? I don't want to alert anyone to our presence."

"Let's go in Jason's office to talk. When we're out of sight they'll be quiet."

Since that's where Caleb wanted to go anyway, he turned again to the door. Moving silently, he twisted the knob and pushed the door open. Nothing moved inside, and he heard no sound. Still, he tiptoed and, when Mrs. Fairmont had closed the door behind her, didn't raise his voice above a low whisper.

"I have a friend who does building inspections, and he says there's an underground room below this office." He watched her face carefully. "Are you saying you don't know about it?"

Guileless round eyes returned his gaze. She shook her head. "I wasn't here when the office was built. I spent a month in Europe with my sister that spring. The kennel was under construction when I left— they hadn't begun this part yet." Bitterness flooded her face. "But I wouldn't be surprised if Richard had a secret room constructed. It would explain why he spent so much time in the pool house at night. I knew he had a mistress, but I didn't dream he would bring her here, to my home."

"Mistress?"

"That girl's mother, of course." Pain appeared in her eyes and the corners of her mouth drooped. "She's probably not been kidnapped at all. If she's here, she probably only wanted to see the place where her father and mother met to carry on their illicit affair."

Now Caleb understood. Sympathy came over him

for this woman who thought her husband had betrayed her. Darcie might not appreciate him telling her secret, but Mrs. Fairmont needed to know the truth.

"Your husband wasn't Darcie's father," he said gently. "He was her uncle. His brother raped her mother."

Horror descended on her face, but was that a touch of relief he spied? It would be natural, if so.

She spoke wonderingly. "So Richard wasn't having an affair with Beth Wiley?"

"No. He was taking care of his brother's daughter and her mother."

"And all this time I thought…" She raked her fingers through her hair. "And you say Darcie has been kidnapped and is being held here?" She looked around. "Where?"

"I don't know." Urgency gripped Caleb's insides like steel bands constricting his lungs. He saw nothing unusual in the room. Four plain walls, one with a windowed door leading to the kennel. Another door in the inside wall, this one without a window, probably opened onto the pool house.

He laid an ear against the wood and heard nothing but silence.

"You should go back to your house and wait until the police arrive," he told Mrs. Fairmont.

"I'm going with you," she replied, her tone stubborn.

Caleb didn't have time to argue with her. Every

minute wasted might be one of Darcie's last. He twisted the handle and opened the door a half inch, listening for sound. Nothing. Placing an eye over the crack, he edged it open further. The room beyond the door lay in darkness, but from somewhere out of sight came a dim glow.

The hinges creaked once as he eased the door open enough to slip through. He stopped, listening intently. Was that the faint sound of voices? He couldn't be sure, but they didn't sound alarmed, so he stepped through and onto a tile-covered floor. Placing his booted feet carefully so as not to make a sound, he went to the center of the room. Mrs. Fairmont followed, her bedroom slippers moving silently after him.

White wicker furniture with brightly patterned cushions faced the sliding glass doors that led to the pool deck. The curtains had been drawn closed, but a faint light shone around the edges. Against the left wall was the rounded countertop island of a wet bar. At first Caleb thought the dim light he'd spied came from the curtains, but he now saw the true source. A closet door stood partially open, and the light came from there.

With a raised hand, he indicated that Mrs. Fairmont should stay back, and he crept to the closet. That was also the source of the muffled voice he heard. He peeked inside.

Turning his head toward Mrs. Fairmont, he mouthed the word, *Bingo*.

A carpeted panel in the floor had been raised to reveal a set of stairs leading downward. The voice, a man's, carried up the stairs. He strained to make out the words but couldn't.

In the next moment, his heart leaped. A different voice spoke, a female's. Darcie! Hers, he recognized.

Okay, Lord. What do I do now?

A thud behind him interrupted the silence. He whirled around to find Mrs. Fairmont watching him through rounded eyes. At her feet was a book she had apparently knocked off a table. She mouthed, *Sorry.*

The mumbling voice below stopped.

Caleb dashed toward her. If they'd heard below, they would come to investigate. He snatched the book off the floor and hustled Mrs. Fairmont into the only hiding place available, behind the wet bar. They crouched together, listening for sounds of approach, Caleb in the front and her huddled against the back corner. She raised her arm and shoved the gun toward him. Though he hated the things with a passion, he took it.

Lord, please don't let me have to use this.

TWENTY-TWO

Horror spread through Darcie's chest, robbing her of breath. She was standing in front of a murderer. And he had a gun pointed at her.

She cleared her throat. "Why?"

"Purely by accident. Lewis discovered the lab last year, and he started blackmailing Richard right away. His demands were becoming increasingly bothersome, so Richard asked me to talk to him. But Lewis was an idiot, and irritating as well. We argued. He took a swing at me." Mitchell shrugged. "The situation escalated, and the next thing I knew—"

A noise from above interrupted his confession. Mitchell's head jerked upward, as did Butch's.

"Mike can't have gotten there and back this quickly," Mitchell whispered. "Check it out."

Butch went to the same drawer Mitchell had a moment before and withdrew another pistol. Moving quietly, he crept toward the stairs, his eye fixed on the ceiling. When he got to the bottom of the stairway, he whispered over his shoulder, "That idiot left the hatch open."

Mitchell lunged forward and grabbed Darcie. He held her in place with one hand and placed the gun barrel to her temple. "One sound and you're dead. Understand?"

Heart pounding, she nodded.

Butch doused the lights, and the room went pitch-black. The pressure on her arm tightened, and the gun pressed against her skull. Butch made almost no sound as he climbed the stairs. In the minutes that followed, Darcie had a wild desire to pray. It might do no good, but she couldn't stop herself.

Dear God, I don't want to die. Is there somebody up there trying to rescue me? Help me! Please, please help me!

Not eloquent for sure, but that was the best she could do under the circumstances. She repeated her plea over and over in her mind.

Finally, she heard a door close above and then the light came back on. Butch's legs appeared, paused as he lowered the panel over the staircase and then descended the rest of the way. Darcie's sharp disappointment found release in a sob.

"Nothing up there at all. Must have been outside."

"You didn't check outside?"

Butch awarded him with a disbelieving scowl. "With that maniac dog running around? No way. I looked out the windows, though. Everything's quiet."

Mitchell released Darcie, and she wasted no time putting a few feet of distance between them. She would take a maniac dog over a maniac murderer anytime. "Was killing my uncle Richard a mistake, too?"

His smile made her shiver. "No mistake. After the incident with Lewis, Richard became difficult. Seems he didn't trust me anymore."

Hmm, I wonder why? Darcie kept her face clear of the sarcastic thought.

"He got scared. Said it was time to close up shop. He wanted me to dismantle the lab and then leave. Offered me money to leave the country and start a new life." A scowl twisted his lips. "The amount was a drop in the bucket compared to what he had, and I told him so. He refused to give me any more."

"So you killed him over money?"

"Oh, no. He never intended to let me leave, I knew that. As soon as I had cleared all the evidence out of this place he would have turned me over to the cops. Not directly, that's not how he worked, but he would have gotten it done." A cold smile came over his face. "That's where you came in."

Her courage frozen in the face of that insane smile, Darcie couldn't manage an answer.

"I knew about you, of course. I'd delivered money to your mother often enough, and then there was that stupid mistake with you getting one of our special collars." He aimed a glare at Butch. "And I knew about the will. At first I was going to kidnap you and use you as leverage to convince Richard to see things my way, so I had Butch and Mike mimic the rapists who've been attacking women in parking lots. But they screwed that up, too." He shook his head in Butch's direction. "Then when you called the other day wanting to meet with your uncle, I realized that was my chance. You almost ruined everything by bringing that big goofball with you."

Darcie would have bristled at the insult to Caleb, but her fear overrode any other reactions.

"But it worked out okay in the end. I was hiding in one of those cubicles, watching, so I knew you were alone with Richard. It was an easy matter to wait until you two left and then…"

His hands made a twisting motion, and Darcie's stomach lurched.

"Is—is that what you're going to do to me?"

The smile took on a plastic sympathy. "Don't worry. I'm getting better at it. And you have a few more hours. I need to wait until tomorrow, when Olivia returns from her sister's. By then we'll have the equipment moved and there won't be any evidence that there was ever anything going on here except an unfaithful, vengeful wife who couldn't stand the thought of her husband's illegitimate child inheriting."

His plan became clear. He intended to pin the murders on Mrs. Fairmont.

When the thug had disappeared behind the closet door, Mrs. Fairmont whispered, "What are we going to do?"

Caleb's thoughts were flying so fast he could barely keep up. One thing was certain, though. He had to get her to safety.

"I want you to sneak out of here, get in your car and leave. On the way, call Detective Samuels and tell him what's going on."

"But what about you?"

"I'm not leaving Darcie down there. Somehow I've got to rescue her."

"Don't you think you should let the police do that?"

He made no answer. What he *should* do didn't enter into the equation. Darcie was in danger, and he wasn't going to leave her there.

"You don't know how many of them are down there," she pointed out in a reasonable tone. "There's no other way in or out except that closet, so there's no way to get to her without them seeing."

She was right on all counts. The man who came up to investigate the noise had spoken to someone else when he came upstairs, and the voice had been lower in timbre than the previous voice. So that meant there were at least two men down there with Darcie. Maybe more.

A distraction might draw them out. Another sound, maybe? Then when the one came to investigate, he could grab him, take him outside and force some information out of him.

That wouldn't work. When he didn't come back immediately, the other one might realize something had gone wrong. He might hurt Darcie, or even use her as a hostage so he could get away. Caleb would be left standing here, watching her taken away to who knew where. And hostages rarely survived once they'd outlived their usefulness. No, he was going to have to get down in that room somehow.

If he couldn't distract them, maybe he could confuse them, at least momentarily. Long enough for him to get down the stairs, ascertain the situation and take them out. The gun's metal felt warm in his hand. The thought of using it on a human being sickened him. In fact, using it at all sickened him. Even if he'd had a gun back when he was facing that guard dog he wouldn't have—

An idea formed. A crazy idea. He slipped his hand into the nail pouch he still wore tied around his waist.

Twisting around to face Mrs. Fairmont, he whispered, "I have an idea. You're probably not going to like it, but it's all I've got."

"Call Mike and find out how long he's going to be."

Mitchell spoke over his shoulder to Butch. He'd set the gun on the countertop and knelt in front of the safe. So far he'd filled a dozen little bags with emeralds, but apparently there were more trays in the safe.

Darcie, seated in one of the folding chairs beside the card table, noted the location of the gun dully. It was on the other side of the room. If she was closer and her hands weren't still bound with duct tape, she might have attempted to go for it. But she'd be stopped before she was even out of the chair.

"Okay." Standing behind her, Butch pulled out a cell phone and glanced at the screen. "Stupid phone. I can never get a decent signal down here unless I'm near the stairs."

He crossed the room to stand beside the exposed staircase, his phone pointed upward, and punched a number.

Suddenly he looked up at the door. "Wait a minute. I think he's back. The closet just opened."

Still squatting on the floor, Mitchell's head jerked toward him. "You sure it's Mike?"

Butch pulled the pistol from where he'd tucked it in his waistband and aimed the barrel upward.

"Please, please be careful." Mrs. Fairmont's whisper held a tearful plea.

Caleb glanced at her. Was she worried about him or the fuzzy white dogs she held in her arms? Probably both.

"The minute you put them down, you run like crazy. Call the detective, and then lock yourself in a bathroom or something and don't make a sound. Promise?"

She nodded.

He broke off a couple of pieces of hot dog and gave one to each of the dogs she held. They gobbled the treat. The rest of the wiener he tore into little pieces and stooped to feed the eager puppies that danced around his feet. It had taken a few tries before they'd recognized the morsels as food, because they'd never eaten anything except puppy chow and mother's milk. But after watching their parents devour their treats, they'd been willing to give them a try. Now they begged enthusiastically for more.

Caleb straightened and held Mrs. Fairmont's gaze. "Time to go."

The breath she heaved shuddered, whether with nerves or tears, he couldn't tell. She whispered something softly to the two bigger dogs she held and then bent over to set them on the floor. Removing the last three wieners from the package, Caleb waved them in the faces of the dogs to make sure he had their attention while their owner left the room.

When she had disappeared through the door to the office, he held the gun in his right hand and opened the closet door with his left, all the while dangling the wieners just out of the dogs' reach. A couple of the puppies barked a demand. "Yes, these are for you. All you have to do is go get them."

With the hand holding the gun, he found the ring in the carpeted floor panel and lifted. In the same motion, he swung the wieners in front of the dog's noses and tossed them down the stairs.

The result was exactly what he'd hoped. A moving mound of white fur tumbled down the stairs after the hot dogs, a dozen canine voices barking a joyful pursuit.

The exclamation he heard from downstairs was music to his ears. It came from a man standing close by. Without hesitating, Caleb leaped after the puppies.

Darcie felt the release of pressure in the room more than heard the hatch being thrown open. The familiar sound of yapping dogs didn't at first register. That noise had no place here, no frame of reference. She caught sight of what looked like a furry boulder tumbling down the stairs at the same moment Butch shouted in surprise.

When she saw Caleb's legs appear, she jumped out of her seat and ran. An explosion assaulted her ears. A gunshot. *Caleb!* She couldn't stop to see what had happened. Ears ringing, she barely heard the puppies' frightened cries as she continued her charge across the room.

She slammed into Mitchell as his fingers closed on the handle of his gun.

"You stupid—"

His sentence ended in a scream when Darcie, hands still bound behind her back, fought with the only weapon she had. Her teeth sank into the tender flesh where shoulder gave way to neck. The coppery taste of blood filled her mouth.

Still screaming, Mitchell lifted the pistol and smashed it into her head, while at the same time bucking his body. Dazed, Darcie released her bite and was thrown backward onto the floor. Horrified, she saw him turn, the pistol in his hand.

"Darcie, get the gun!"

Caleb's command preceded his attack. He flew across the floor and launched himself at Mitchell. Horrified, she watched as Caleb jerked Mitchell's arm backward, heard the audible snap as it connected with the edge of the counter. The room was filled with a second loud noise: Mitchell's screams. Caleb took the gun from his unresisting hand and looked at her.

Then Darcie understood. He hadn't meant for her to get Mitchell's gun, but Butch's.

She jerked around and spied the weapon in the middle of the floor, where it had landed when Caleb jumped down the stairs onto the man's back. She struggled to her knees, her movements awkward without the use of her hands, and started to crawl across the floor.

Too late.

Butch had recovered from the momentary surprise of having two hundred and twenty pounds worth of man leap on him from above. He hefted himself up onto his knees and lunged forward.

His hand landed on the weapon.

Darcie froze as he lifted the gun and pointed the barrel straight at Caleb.

"Put the guns down." Butch shouted to make himself heard over Mitchell's screams of pain.

Caleb looked at her, and she saw defeat in his eyes.

A sob rose in her throat and threatened to choke her. His movements slow, Caleb, who held a gun in each hand, stretched his arms toward the countertop.

"You do the same," came another voice from the stairs.

Darcie looked up to see Detective Samuels descending the stairway, his own weapon held in both hands and trained on Butch. Four police officers followed him down, each armed with a service weapon and a grim expression that proclaimed they would not hesitate to use them.

Tight-lipped, Butch lowered his gun and shoved it across the floor.

As the room filled with policemen, Caleb hurried over to drop to his knees behind her. Darcie didn't try to stop the sobs that racked her body as he ripped through the duct tape to free her. The moment she could move her hands, she spun and threw her arms around him.

"You came for me," she sobbed. "I thought I was going to die, but you came for me."

His arms circled her and pulled her close. "I promised I would keep you safe." His lips pressed against her hair, her ear, her cheek, and she realized he was kissing her and praying at the same time. "Thank You for keeping her safe."

"How did you get here so quickly?" Caleb asked Samuels. "The judge must have signed that warrant in record time."

They were seated at the same poolside table where the detective had questioned them the first time. This time the pool glowed with underwater lights and cricket songs rose into the night sky from somewhere in the landscaping plants. Beside Caleb, Darcie had scooted her chair close so she could keep a firm grip on his hand. The warmth generated by their intertwined fingers had nothing to do with the nighttime temperature and everything to do with the deep sense of joy that sang louder than the crickets in Caleb's heart.

"I suppose he has by now," Samuels answered. "I sent another detective to his house when I got the call to come here."

"Call?" Caleb looked at Mrs. Fairmont. "I didn't think you'd even had time to get back to your house, much less make the call."

She looked embarrassed. "I called 911 earlier, before I came to investigate whatever was disturbing the dogs at the kennel. With all the excitement, I forgot to mention that."

"As soon as I heard the call over the radio, I knew who it was." Samuels scowled at him. "I should have locked you up."

An officer approached the table. "Detective, we've got all the photos we need, and we're ready to start hauling out the equipment. You want to come take a look before we move it?"

Samuels jerked a nod and stood. Before he left, he speared Caleb with a final glare. "You're lucky you didn't get yourself and Ms. Wiley killed." The glare softened into something that might be interpreted as grudging respect. "But good job."

When he'd disappeared into the pool house, Mrs. Fairmont turned to Darcie.

"I owe you an apology. I thought…" She lowered her gaze to the hands folded in her lap. "Well, never mind what I thought. I was wrong. I hope you'll forgive me for treating you badly. And your poor mother." She shook her head. "I would have helped her, if only I'd known."

The smile Darcie gave her was tender. "I know you would have, Mrs. Fairmont."

"Please call me Olivia." She looked up and met Darcie's gaze. "And I hope we can be friends. After all, you're the last of the Fairmonts. From Richard's last words to you, I'd like to think he intended to tell me the truth about your parentage, and that we would both acknowledge you as family. I would like that still."

Tears sparkled on Darcie's lashes. "Thank you."

Mrs. Fairmont heaved a sigh and stood. "I have a feeling the police will be here until daylight, and I won't be able to sleep a wink after all this excitement anyway. I think I'll make coffee." She left and disappeared into the house.

Finally alone with Darcie, Caleb was attacked by a sudden shyness. There was so much he wanted to say to her, but there were no words to give shape to his thoughts. They sat in silence for a long moment, his entire being focused on the feel of her hand in his.

She broke the silence with a whisper. "I thought I was going to die down in that room."

"Shhh." He squeezed her hand. "It's over. You're safe now. Don't think about it."

"No, I want to think about it." She turned in her chair to face him. "I thought I was going to die, and that was scary. But then something even scarier happened. When that man pointed the gun at you, I thought *you* were going to die." Tears filled her eyes. "I couldn't bear it if anything happened to you."

The words touched his heart and sank into his soul. Did she mean what he thought she meant? Holding her gaze in his, he rose, pulling her up with him.

"Darcie, are you saying—" He stopped. He couldn't be that fortunate.

"I'm saying I love you, Caleb Buchanan." She released his hand, but only to slide hers up his arm and around his neck. "And I'm hoping—" Starlight twinkled in the eyes that looked into his. "I'm *praying* that you love me, too."

He had only one answer for that. He lowered his lips to hers and gave himself over to proving that he did.

EPILOGUE

"And now, by the power vested in me by the state of Georgia and in the name of the Lord Jesus Christ, I pronounce you husband and wife." The minister beamed at Caleb. "Mr. Buchanan, you may kiss your bride."

"With pleasure," Caleb answered, and swept Darcie into his arms for their first married kiss.

While the small audience clapped, Darcie surrendered to her husband's embrace. Music rang in her heart as she felt her feet leave the ground, swept up in his powerful arms. Mrs. Caleb Buchanan. She never wanted this moment to end.

"Dude, enough," Mason said over Caleb's shoulder. "There's a cake to be cut."

Caleb and Darcie broke apart, laughing.

"All right, all right," he told his groomsman. "We don't want you passing out from hunger and spoiling our wedding."

"Actually, it's me who might faint from hunger," Karina said as she hugged Darcie. "This baby obviously has his father's appetite."

Smiling, Darcie laid a hand on Karina's bulging belly. "Well, let's get him fed. There's enough food at the reception to feed half of Atlanta. Aunt Olivia made sure of that."

"Nothing but the best for my niece's wedding." Olivia looked dazzling today, her eyes sparkling nearly as much as the diamonds that glittered on her neck and earlobes. She addressed the dozen or so wedding guests seated in chairs on the Fairmont Estate lawn. "The wedding party will be busy with the photographer for a few moments. I invite you to go inside and help yourselves to *hors d' oeuvres.* Dinner will be served in thirty minutes."

The guests rose and began making their way toward the house. Cordelia Gates caught Darcie's eye and waggled her fingers before falling in with the others. Officer Jarron Roberts grinned at the wedding party and then offered his arm to Sloane's mother, with whom he seemed quite taken. The child lagged behind, her gaze straying toward the Fairmont Kennel, and Darcie knew she was looking for an excuse to disappear for a few minutes. The desire to see the birthplace of her precious Purdy was too strong for an eleven-year-old to resist.

Olivia had been horrified to discover that some of her "babies" had ended up in dog shelters after their owners removed the jewels from the special collars. She'd hired someone to locate every puppy sold since launching her Maltipom business six years ago and at last had ascertained that those who went to shelters did eventually end up in loving homes, like Sloane's Purdy.

The last of the guests filed away and the photographer started rearranging his tripods. Olivia gave Darcie a quick hug and then hurried away, mumbling something about checking on the caterers.

"I hope they have crackers," said Lauren as she, too, embraced the bride. "I don't think I can stomach anything else."

Brent slipped an arm around his wife's still-slender waist. "If they don't, I'll go get you some. Anything for the mother of my child."

Mason clapped Caleb on the shoulder. "You two are going to have to hurry if you want to catch up with us in the kid department."

Darcie's new husband turned pink. "I don't…that is, we aren't…" He looked at her, a plea for help plain on his face.

She smiled at him. Someday they would celebrate their love with the addition of a child, but not yet. "We're not in a hurry. We'll have fun being aunt and uncle to your babies for a while."

Caleb nodded. "Besides, we have Percy and Mickey and Minnie to keep us busy."

Brent shook his head, chuckling. "I still can't believe you, of all people, are going to share a house with *three* dogs."

"Hey, they're cool, okay? Besides, they're more like smart, hairy guinea pigs than dogs."

Darcie joined in the laughter. Aunt Olivia had insisted on giving them two Fairmont designer puppies as a wedding gift. Caleb had grown attached to Percy in the six months since they had met and had showed real enthusiasm when he picked his puppy out of the litter. She glanced toward the kennel, which had been repaired after the demolition to retrieve Uncle Kenneth's "insurance" from inside one of the walls. Under the threat of increased prison time, he'd confessed to hiding copies of Uncle Richard's ledgers, which listed the names of his Colombian contacts and those U.S. citizens who purchased illegally imported emeralds before he'd started creating synthesized ones. They'd also found a tidy cache of gemstones.

Lauren tilted her head, a thoughtful expression on her face. "You know, God has done something really awesome in this little group."

Karina nodded. "I was thinking the same thing earlier. We were all brought together because of false accusations and lies, but He helped us uncover the truth."

Caleb slipped an arm around Darcie's waist and pulled her close. "And the truth has set us free."

Free. Darcie looked up into the eyes of her husband and saw love shining there. She had truly been set free, and not just from her ordeal in the underground room. She'd been freed from the hurts of her past, from the secrets that had brought her shame and made her afraid to trust. Free to live, to love and to look forward to a joyful future with the man she loved.

* * * * *

Dear Reader,

Every so often a character comes along who really resonates with the author and readers. Caleb Buchanan is one of those characters. As I wrote the first two books in the Falsely Accused series, I fell in love with this muscle-bound, tattoo-covered tough guy with a heart for the downtrodden and hurting. I've lost count of the number of letters I've received saying, "I can't wait for Caleb's story." Oh, the pressure! I didn't want to disappoint anyone by writing a story that didn't show Caleb as the fascinating man we came to know and love in DANGEROUS IMPOSTOR and BULLSEYE. I shouldn't have worried. Once I got the first few chapters in shape, the rest of the story fell in place because Caleb is such a wonderful man to spend time with.

And what a hoot to pit him against a litter of fluffy white puppies. Can't you just picture that great big man with all those puppies leaping around his feet? I laugh every time I think of that scene.

I hope you enjoyed this story. I'd love to know what you think! Contact me through www.VirginiaSmith. org, or become my friend on Facebook at http://www. facebook.com/ginny.p.smith. Or you can write to me: Virginia Smith, P.O. Box 70271, West Valley City, Utah 84170. I love receiving letters from book lovers!

Virginia Smith

Questions for Discussion

1. When the book opens, Darcie has just lost her mother. Why did she move to Atlanta so quickly after her mother's death?

2. What is Darcie's reaction to Caleb when they first meet? Do you think his tattoos impacted her initial reaction?

3. Darcie is single and alone, without friends. Why is she reluctant to enter into a relationship with Caleb?

4. Caleb is also single and alone, and his first reaction to Darcie is to help her. What happens to change his mind?

5. When Darcie calls Caleb at home and asks him to come over to her apartment, he refuses. Why?

6. Mrs. Fairmont makes no attempt to hide her dislike of Darcie. How does that dislike affect the detective's opinion of her? Was he correct to question Darcie's claims?

7. What would you say is Caleb's strongest characteristic? How does that strength affect him throughout the course of the story?

8. Do you prefer cats over dogs, or vice versa? Why?

9. Who were your suspects throughout the book?

10. Who is your favorite character in this book?

11. When Darcie discovers the secret of her mother's past, she is angry and upset but also feels ashamed. Is her reaction normal?

12. Caleb tries to comfort her by quoting a Scripture that most of us have heard many times: *We know that all things work together for good to them that love God, to them who are called according to His purpose* (Romans 8:28). Do you think his interpretation of that Scripture is accurate?

13. Were you aware of synthetic gemstones before reading this book? (Check out Chatham Created Gems, Inc., to learn more about man-made gems.)

14. If you read all three books in the Falsely Accused series, with which of the characters did you identify most?

15. Was the Epilogue a satisfying ending to the Falsely Accused series? Why or why not?

LARGER-PRINT BOOKS!

GET 2 FREE
LARGER-PRINT NOVELS
PLUS 2 FREE
MYSTERY GIFTS

Love Inspired®
SUSPENSE
RIVETING INSPIRATIONAL ROMANCE

Larger-print novels are now available...

YES! Please send me 2 FREE LARGER-PRINT Love Inspired® Suspense novels and my 2 FREE mystery gifts (gifts are worth about $10). After receiving them, if I don't wish to receive any more books, I can return the shipping statement marked "cancel." If I don't cancel, I will receive 4 brand-new novels every month and be billed just $4.99 per book in the U.S. or $5.49 per book in Canada. That's a savings of at least 23% off the cover price. It's quite a bargain! Shipping and handling is just 50¢ per book in the U.S. and 75¢ per book in Canada.* I understand that accepting the 2 free books and gifts places me under no obligation to buy anything. I can always return a shipment and cancel at any time. Even if I never buy another book, the two free books and gifts are mine to keep forever.

110/310 IDN FVZ7

Name _____ (PLEASE PRINT)

Address _____ Apt. #

City _____ State/Prov. _____ Zip/Postal Code

Signature (if under 18, a parent or guardian must sign)

Mail to the Harlequin® Reader Service:
IN U.S.A.: P.O. Box 1867, Buffalo, NY 14240-1867
IN CANADA: P.O. Box 609, Fort Erie, Ontario L2A 5X3

**Are you a current subscriber to Love Inspired Suspense books
and want to receive the larger-print edition?
Call 1-800-873-8635 or visit www.ReaderService.com.**

* Terms and prices subject to change without notice. Prices do not include applicable taxes. Sales tax applicable in N.Y. Canadian residents will be charged applicable taxes. Offer not valid in Quebec. This offer is limited to one order per household. Not valid for current subscribers to Love Inspired Suspense larger print books. All orders subject to credit approval. Credit or debit balances in a customer's account(s) may be offset by any other outstanding balance owed by or to the customer. Please allow 4 to 6 weeks for delivery. Offer available while quantities last.

Your Privacy—The Harlequin® Reader Service is committed to protecting your privacy. Our Privacy Policy is available online at www.ReaderService.com or upon request from the Harlequin Reader Service.

We make a portion of our mailing list available to reputable third parties that offer products we believe may interest you. If you prefer that we not exchange your name with third parties, or if you wish to clarify or modify your communication preferences, please visit us at www.ReaderService.com/consumerchoice or write to us at Harlequin Reader Service Preference Service, P.O. Box 9062, Buffalo, NY 14269. Include your complete name and address.

LISLPDIR13

SUSPENSE

RIVETING INSPIRATIONAL ROMANCE

Watch for our series of edge-
of-your-seat suspense novels.
These contemporary tales
of intrigue and romance
feature Christian characters
facing challenges to their faith...
and their lives!

**AVAILABLE IN REGULAR
& LARGER-PRINT FORMATS**

For exciting stories that reflect traditional values,
visit:

www.ReaderService.com

LISUSDIR11B

ReaderService.com

Manage your account online!

- Review your order history
- Manage your payments
- Update your address

*We've designed
the Harlequin® Reader Service
website just for you.*

Enjoy all the features!

- Reader excerpts from any series
- Respond to mailings and
  special monthly offers
- Discover new series available to you
- Browse the Bonus Bucks catalog
- Share your feedback

Visit us at:
ReaderService.com

RS13